Sleigh Bells
ON BREAD LOAF
MOUNTAIN

Other Books by Lindy Miller

The Magic Ingredient (A Bar Harbor Holiday Novel, Book 1)

Lindy Miller and Terence Brody
Aloha with Love

Forthcoming From Rosewind Books

Lindy Miller
Mistletoe Magic (A Bar Harbor Holiday Novel, Book 2)

Sleigh Bells
ON BREAD LOAF
MOUNTAIN

LINDY MILLER

ROSEWIND

Sleigh Bells on Bread Loaf Mountain

Cover design by Qamber Designs and Media
www.QamberDesignsandMedia.com

ISBN: 978-1-64548-078-5

Published by Rosewind Romance
An imprint of Vesuvian Books
www.RosewindRomance.com

Printed in the United States

10 9 8 7 6 5 4 3 2 1

Dedicated to everyone who hears the sound of sleigh bells in the snow. And to my grandmothers, who kept our holiday home warm, joyful, and brimming with sweets.

Chapter One

"You're *seriously* going to drive all the way to Vermont to spend Christmas with family you haven't seen in years?"

Spencer's voice was so thick with sarcasm Roxanne couldn't decide which part of what he'd said offended him the most.

Her work bestie slumped dramatically against the high wall of her cubicle, fanning at himself. The perfection of his coiffed hair and meticulously starched clothes might have given the impression that Spencer Chen was impervious to the indignities of human emotion, but the expression on his face said plainly he was not. At the present, he was wearing the most severe of his trademark histrionic faces: upper lip drawn back to expose a row of pearly white teeth, nostrils flared, expertly sculpted eyebrows arched. The look said he hated everything that had just come out of his mouth.

All of it.

Don't encourage him. Roxanne bit her lip and willed herself to stay silent. When Spencer got on a roll, it was best to just let him tire himself out. Working in the fashion industry had earned her a closet full of designer labels and, along with them, the kid gloves necessary to handle the drama queens in her life, including

Spencer. Usually, Roxanne enjoyed his dramatic reactions to everyday happenings—so long as they weren't directed at her.

Like now.

She opened her mouth to speak, but Spencer wasn't finished.

"In a *log* cabin," he added, stabbing his index finger upward to punctuate each word. A shudder passed through his body as he dropped his palm over his heart. He was so spun up he actually looked faint.

"I am." Roxanne drew her response out and bit her lip. Maybe if she said the words slowly, they wouldn't spin him back up.

Spencer closed his eyes and sucked his teeth, still fanning.

She sighed. "It's not as bad as you're making it sound, though, Spence. Seriously."

"Oh, honey." Spencer's eyes snapped open with an exaggerated pop. "It *absolutely* is. You're *Divine*, remember? Being divine isn't just a job; it's a lifestyle. And there's nothing cute about spending the biggest holiday of the year in the sticks."

"I know. I don't like it either. Trust me, I didn't move to New York and get a job at the hottest fashion magazine in the industry only to go running back to play dress-up in the mountains." She felt a pang of guilt. Once upon a time, she'd loved spending the holidays at her family's cabin, but that had been a very long time ago, and life was different now than it was then. "But it's Christmas, and my family wants me to come home."

Spencer pursed his lips and blinked hard, preparing to make a point. "Okay, here's the tea. It's not just Christmas—it's *timing*. In the past two years, you've leapfrogged from copy desk to editor to running your own feature." He spoke in stilted tones, intentionally leaving space between each word. "You've attended

Milan Fashion Week. You wowed the team with a spread of the royal wedding. Vivian Yurich—*the* Vivian Yurich, *Divine*'s goddess of an editor-in-chief—knows you by *name*. She's had your designs on her desk. You're on the fast-catwalk to making a real name for yourself."

She shrugged. It would take more than a list of bullet points on her résumé to make Roxanne feel like she'd accomplished anything more than try to keep up with a job she still wasn't sure how she'd managed to land.

Spencer waited for a beat, then rolled his eyes when she didn't respond and clicked his tongue. "To sum up, you have better things to do than go play mountain girl for the holidays. You need to be *here*, ringing in the season in the City and schmoozing the holiday crowd. Making connections. Toasting champagne in Rockefeller Plaza with everyone who's anyone. I'm sure your family would understand that, even if it *is* Christmas. The holidays happen every year, but these types of career once-in-a-lifetimes don't come along every day."

Roxanne tugged at her skirt again, then reached to fidget with the miniature ceramic tree on her desk—the only evidence of the impending holiday she'd allowed in her workspace. It might have been snowy out, all the department store windows filled with whimsical winter displays, but other than the small tree, it was business as usual in Roxanne's cubicle. If she wanted holiday spirit, she could take in whatever seasonal music was playing downstairs in the lobby.

"It all sounds so impressive when you say it like that, but I'm not the only editor at *Divine* hoping for their big break—present company included." Roxanne considered the sea of cubicles around her, all stationed with high-fashion hopefuls. "In fact, I'm pretty sure I remember it being part of the job description."

"Speaking of our glamorous leader-in-chief," Spencer continued, returning back to the thread of his earlier remark as if he hadn't heard her, "have you heard anything back on the new designs you gave her?"

Roxanne's skirt suddenly felt too tight. "Not yet, and I'm trying not to feel down about it." She'd rather listen to Spencer yammer on about the indignities of spending the holidays roughing it in the mountains than talk about her latest design sketches. At least arguing about her schedule kept her mind off wondering why she hadn't heard anything—or worst, what she *might* hear. The last designs she'd summoned up the courage to show Vivian had been passed off as "too Plain Jane" for the runway elite, and while Roxanne hoped she'd done a better job of hitting the target this time around, her stomach had been in knots ever since she handed over her sketches. Spencer talked about career once-in-a-lifetimes, but Roxanne wasn't even sure her career was headed in the right direction. Plain Jane. Sure, high fashion was a mark above the typical wardrobe, but shouldn't people be entitled to feel fashionable every day? "Maybe it's a good thing. Vivian isn't exactly known for sugarcoating her feedback."

Spencer pursed his lips and flicked his eyelids in an impatient flutter. "That explains the new hairstyle."

If there was one person who could sniff out a sensitive subject, it was Spencer Chen. And if there was a sign someone was in desperate need of a fresh start, it was a spontaneous trip to the salon.

"Do you like it?" Roxanne resisted the urge to fidget.

Spencer dismissed the question with a flippant twist of his wrist. "Of course, I like it. Francesca does great work. There's nobody else I'd even consider letting touch my hair."

"I wasn't sure about the bangs." She stuffed her fingers under her thighs.

"Bangs are making a comeback." He shrugged. "Besides, they make your cheekbones pop. Very *Divine*, and not only in the lifestyle way. You're a burgeoning fashionista, Roxanne Hudson, totally on trend—which is *why* I can't believe you're going to run off to the woods for Christmas, instead of staying here with your fancy new hair and celebrating in style with me."

"Vermont really isn't as bad as you make it sound." Roxanne peeled her hands out from beneath her and turned her attention to the stack of fabric swatches waiting on her desk. "It'll be very Currier and Ives," she went on, but the reference sounded old-fashioned coming out of her lips, and she paused to reconsider. "Or maybe Martha Stewart. *Post*-prison Martha Stewart."

The last was an important clarification. Pre-jail Martha Stewart had been DIY and Kmart; post-jail Martha Stewart was DIY and Snoop Dogg—edgier and several degrees of magnitude more *en vogue* by every possible metric. Neither was terribly high fashion, but holiday decorating had its own rules. Even kitschy could come off chic if you sold it right.

"Rox. *Honey.*" Spencer settled himself against the edge of her desk with a tsk, careful not to crease his perfectly pressed rose-colored shirt. He fixed her with a glower that was half-concerned and half-judgmental. "Vermont. Road trip. Awkward family reunions." He widened his eyes meaningfully. "You hate all of those things, and rightly so—they're *dreadful*. Why on earth are

5

you doing this to yourself? Spill the tea."

Collecting her thoughts, Roxanne set the fabric swatches on her desk. She righted their corners, smoothed her thin cashmere sweater against her chest, and flipped the ends of her recently trimmed hair over her shoulder as she turned a defiant face to her coworker-slash-bestie.

"Because it's Christmas," she declared. "It's the season of giving, and"—Roxanne sighed, already exhausted from trying to hide her true feelings from someone who would see through her act anyway—"perpetual suffering. This year I'm giving up what's left of my sanity and spending the holidays in the woods."

"Honey, you do realize Santa comes in, like, *three* days. We don't even have time to throw your sanity a goodbye brunch. Tell me the real reason you're missing the biggest holiday parties of the year." Spencer's lips pursed. "You do realize Christmas is the *only* time outside of a wedding it's acceptable to wear white after Labor Day?"

The corner of Roxanne's mouth tightened. Three days. In all honesty, she should have left already. The longer she postponed her departure, the more likely it became she'd lose her nerve and not go at all, which only made her more anxious. "I haven't spent the holidays at home since college, but I figured I'd put in the face time with the family," she fibbed. "Enjoy the peace and quiet?"

Spencer scoffed and flicked a speck of invisible lint off his sleeve. "Mm. It sounds so …" His voice trailed off and his lips puckered while he searched for the right term. He wrinkled his nose as if whatever he'd decided on actually tasted bad. "*Quaint.*"

The word was so sharp it hurt Roxanne's ears.

"It's for my Grandma Myrtle," Roxanne confessed, dropping

her voice to a conspiratorial whisper. "She hasn't been doing well and her doctors say she isn't going to get better. This might be her last Christmas, and she wants the family to spend it together. Grandma Myrtle was always the one who believed in me most—I wouldn't even be in fashion, much less at *Divine*, if it wasn't for her encouraging me every step of the way. Spending the holidays together may be the last gift I ever get to give her. I can't just not go."

Spencer was unmoved, but Roxanne could see the wheels turning behind his dark amber eyes. "So, why don't you invite your family to spend the holidays here? You can do all the normal touristy stuff—the Rockefeller tree, ice skating in Central Park—but you know, in *civilization*. Then you could still keep up appearances, too. Win-win."

Briefly, Roxanne considered sliding Grandma Myrtle's wheelchair around on the ice but pushed the thought away. "Grandma Myrtle wants everyone to spend Christmas at our family cabin in the *mountains*, not in the City. We used to spend all of our holidays there. It's ... special."

Spencer cocked a disbelieving eyebrow and mouthed the word *special*.

"Come on, Spence. Didn't your family have some silly old holiday traditions when you were growing up?"

As if by magic, Spencer found another piece of lint on his shirt. "*The Nutcracker*, every single year. So tedious. I still have nightmares about the Mouse King."

Roxanne rolled her eyes. Spencer hadn't missed a single performance the entire time she'd known him, and he spent almost as much time at the ballet as he did Manhattan's salons. He'd give his right arm to design a costume for the New York City Ballet.

"Christmas at the cabin was different," she mused. "It was sort of magical out there in the snow. All the trees covered in white. Icicles hanging from the eaves, sparkling in the lights Dad strung around the cabin. Mistletoe and presents under the tree. I'd wait all year to roast chestnuts, make snowmen and snow angels. We'd light a big fire in the fireplace and sing carols around it and drink wassail—"

"I forget you were such a simple country girl before you moved to the City," Spencer teased, cutting into her memories.

Simple country girl. Those were three of Roxanne's least favorite words—and strong enough to bring her out of yesteryear and right back into her sterile cubicle, right along with the echo of *quaint* still ringing in her ears. She corrected her posture. "Christmas is always different when you're a kid. And that was a long time ago, *Mouse King.*"

Spencer pulled a face. "At least tell me this place has indoor plumbing?"

The question made Roxanne laugh as she imagined Spencer prancing through the snow to an outhouse, hair askew and snow flecking his starched collar. "The cabin is old and sort of drafty, but it definitely has indoor plumbing—and definitely does *not* have Wi-Fi." She groaned. "I can only hope I'll have cell service, and that's *if* the weather's decent, but I'm not counting on it. Honestly, I think I'd trade indoor plumbing for Wi-Fi."

After all, she wouldn't be tempted to check her email inbox without internet access.

"No, you wouldn't." Spencer rolled his eyes. "Even I wouldn't make that deal, and I'm practically powered by Wi-Fi."

"But even without Wi-Fi or cell service, I can make it through one holiday offline for my grandmother's sake," Roxanne continued, undeterred. "Maybe even cook up a decent article on rustic seasonal décor or something. Make it trendy. Besides, it's only a couple of days, what's the worst that could happen? It's not like I'll go out there and forget who I am." She reached under her desk and retrieved a rib-stitched cashmere beanie from her bag. "Plus, look what I got. My selfies are going to be *super* cute."

Spencer plucked the hat from her hands and gave it a once over before tossing it back in the bag. "Cute. Speaking of Mousey men, what about Mr. Handsome? Will he be joining you on this homey holiday hoorah in the backwoods of nowhere, or are you guys on another hiatus?"

An uncomfortable twinge cramped Roxanne's stomach as her gaze fell on the framed photograph of her and her on-again, off-again, currently off boyfriend. They'd looked so happy: Hunter in board shorts and a linen button-down, her in a silk scarlet sundress that made the dusky hue of her skin tone shine, both beaming at the camera from inside each other's arms. So much was different now, and the picture had only been taken a few months prior. Roxanne couldn't remember the last time they'd done much of anything together, much less looked happy about it.

"Let's go back to talking about my designs and how scared I am Vivian is going to hate them *again*," Roxanne almost said, but didn't. Instead, she scanned her desk for a distraction, anything to stack, staple, or stamp. Perhaps there was an urgent email requiring her attention or some deadline she'd overlooked. She wanted to talk about Hunter even less than she wanted to talk about driving six hours to spend Christmas in the Wi-Fi-less woods. A sudden chill surged through Roxanne's thin cashmere sweater. She hated the cold. She hated the snow. The whole thing made her want to forget about the holidays altogether.

The same basically applies to Hunter, too, Roxanne thought. Why did she even still have the photo on her desk?

She pushed the frame behind the ceramic tree.

"Hunter is ... not coming." Determined not to see Spencer's expression, Roxanne snatched up a pile of glossy cardstock photographs on her desk, tapped the bottom edges against the desktop, and held them against herself defensively as she pushed to her feet and angled for an escape—both from her coworker and her own thoughts.

"Oh, honey, no."

A manicured hand stopped Roxanne in her tracks, and a clucking sound told her she would not be exiting her cubicle so easily. Spencer knew an escape attempt when he saw one.

"Don't tell me—" A worried tone had replaced his previously saucy one.

"We're off again," Roxanne confirmed with a sigh. "I think it's over for good this time."

Spencer laid a sympathetic hand on the curve of her shoulder. "Honey, this relationship has obviously reached its expiration date. Find yourself someone who will treat you right. Besides, it's not like you can't do better. Hunter Hollister's got the looks, but the boy is as dumb as a box of rocks, and you deserve a man who—"

Groaning, Roxanne cut off Spencer's advice before he could get worked up into another frenzy. Harping on her about her lackluster love life was Spencer's second favorite pastime, right after hounding her about her design goals. She sidestepped her way around him, waving the stack of photos as if she could shoo him away like a nosy puppy.

"We're fine, really," she insisted, then corrected, "*I'm* fine."

"Roxanne Hudson, anyone who uses the word *fine* to describe their love life is in deep, deep trouble."

Roxanne slid out of her cubicle with a sigh, moving toward the copy room at the end of the aisle without bothering to respond. Just like he was right about Vermont, Spencer was right about her relationship—or lack thereof. She and Hunter *were* past their expiration date. They'd been hanging on by a thread for months, and it had long since begun to fray.

She was fine with things being over. Really.

Hunter *was* attractive, but of course he was. Tall, dark, and handsome, the guy was everything that made women swoon for Latino men. But models were all hot; it was *literally* their job. Besides, Hunter wasn't a vapid model stereotype. He was ambitious.

He'd probably date a badger if it would help improve his résumé. Roxanne scoffed. That's how it'd felt at the end, hadn't it? Like they were two different people, living two completely different lives and each too preoccupied with their own agendas to bother worrying over each other. When she thought of it that way, it was kind of amazing they'd managed to stick it out as long as they had.

"Oh, Rox." Spencer's voice came from behind as he detached himself from Roxanne's cubicle wall and began to move in the direction of his own desk. He slung a sly wink over his shoulder. "Maybe you should ask Santa for a new man this Christmas— assuming the big guy in red delivers in Vermont. Maybe he'll bring you a big, strong mountain man."

11

Chapter Two

*C*ome on, Roxanne. You got this. Roxanne laid a sweater in her suitcase and smoothed away the wrinkles. *It's just a couple of days offline at the cabin, no big deal. No one is emailing over the holidays, not even Vivian Yurich.* She lowered the lid of her suitcase and zipped it shut. She finished the last in a mumble. "Besides, it's not like there's anything going on around here to stick around for, no matter what Spencer says."

She wasn't exactly looking forward to this trip, but after the day's conversation with Spencer, the idea of spending the holidays alone in her empty apartment was somehow even less appealing. With Hunter gone, probably for good, and still no news from Vivian, Roxanne could use something to keep her mind off her life. Plus, even if she wasn't thrilled about the drive or the snow or the whole holiday-in-the-woods thing, she was looking forward to seeing her grandmother.

"Christmas isn't Christmas without family." That's what Grandma Myrtle had always said. Roxanne could imagine the old woman as she'd last seen her, standing at the large island in the center of the cabin's kitchen, pouring steaming hot cocoa into snowmen-decorated mugs. "You don't need snow or presents or much of anything else if you've got loved ones to spend the holidays with. That includes yourself, too. The spirit of the season is something you feel on the inside just as much as you experience on the out. Love yourself and those around you and you'll have everything you could ask for at Christmastime."

Her grandmother's wisdom echoing in her ears, Roxanne took an appraising look at herself in the full-length bedroom mirror. She had decided to go vintage with her look, pairing leggings with an oversized chenille cowl-neck sweater, a fleece-lined utility jacket, and cuffed suede knee-high boots. She'd swept her hair to the side, pinned it in place, and added pricey aviator glasses to complete the ensemble. The outfit might not be the warmest thing she'd ever worn, but it looked great.

"A fashion editor should never be caught unaware," Roxanne reminded her reflection. "Besides, you want to look your best when you arrive at the cabin. Really show everyone you know what you're doing, and that you're not wasting your time in New York. Fashion isn't a hobby, it's a job."

Warmer clothes were packed in her suitcase, along with several professionally wrapped gifts Roxanne had bought for family members she didn't have a clue how to buy for. She'd also tucked a bottle of expensive French wine into her shoulder bag, just in case. The members of her immediate family weren't big drinkers, but Roxanne suspected she'd need a glass or two to help her through the next several days. Her sister, Rachel, was bringing her kids, Ella and Ethan. The older of the two, Ella, had recently turned four—or so Roxanne thought. Four sounded about right; she'd been a newborn the last time Roxanne had seen her sister, who'd been pregnant then with Ethan.

Roxanne stared at herself in the mirror and thought about Grandma Myrtle. Maybe the outfit was too much? Pretty wasn't always exactly practical, but it made her feel better—empowered and confident, exactly what she thought fashion should be. "Christmas is about loving yourself and those around you. Got it."

Loving yourself was easy when you liked what you saw in the mirror, regardless of labels. Her reflection grimaced as the pricey boots pinched her toes.

"It's only a couple of days. Family, presents, and then back to business."

Still eyeballing herself in the mirror, Roxanne pulled her phone from her pocket and tapped the contact to ring the lobby. "This is Roxanne Hudson in 31D. Can the valet bring my car up, please?"

"On its way," the man on the other end of the line confirmed.

Her fancy new BMW was waiting for her by the time Roxanne made it to the front of her building. She tipped the valet for loading her luggage before sinking into the cushy leather driver's seat.

Okay, let's see if we can remember how to do this. Roxanne refamiliarized herself with the various buttons and knobs of the car's interior. The cockpit was black, silver, and chrome from chair to console, and had more bells and whistles than were useful, much less necessary. Why had she bought such a fancy car when she never even bothered to drive it?

Roxanne had only driven the car once—the day she'd gotten it. Her last car had been a rusted, old model Mazda hatchback with a manual transmission, a dent in the passenger door, and an AUX outlet she'd had to plug her iPod into. Her new vehicle was sleeker, shinier, and the status symbol she hoped reflected her image since moving to New York. Dress for the job you want and don't forget to accessorize, right? It didn't matter the car sat undriven in her apartment's garage for weeks at a time.

Once she was satisfied with her assessment of the car's formidable command center and felt she remembered what controlled what, Roxanne buckled herself in and verified the gas tank gauge was on full. The drive to the cabin would take six hours, and she didn't want to have to stop any more than absolutely necessary—a grand total of pit stops she hoped equaled zero.

Roxanne had just plugged in the GPS coordinates to the cabin into the car's navigation system and her hand was poised above the gearshift when an unfamiliar ringing alerted her to an incoming call. She fumbled for her cell phone, then remembered the car responded to voice commands. Hands-free driving was safe driving, after all.

"Pick up." That was the correct command, wasn't it? She scrunched her lips. "Hello?"

Hunter's smooth tenor slid through the car's speaker system. "Hey."

Roxanne winced as something in the pit of her stomach twisted. The sound was so clear he could have been sitting in the seat right next to her. Packing had helped push the niggling thoughts about her ex out of her head all morning, but the second she heard his voice they came rushing back. She had to talk around a lump in her throat. "What's up?"

"You don't sound very happy to hear from me."

Roxanne shook her head, then remembered Hunter couldn't see her, no matter how close he sounded. "No, sorry, it's not that at all. I am glad to hear from you, I just didn't *expect* to hear from you." *Especially since we just broke up—again,* she almost added, but didn't. Instead, she said, "Aren't you still on a shoot in Madrid?"

A pause. "I am, but I wanted to call you," he said, then cleared his throat. "Check in, I guess."

Hunter sounded flustered, which loosened the knot in Roxanne's stomach.

"I know we didn't really have any holiday plans or anything, but it looks like we may need an extra couple of days here … some issue with the lighting. And Andrea has food poisoning, so we're behind schedule."

"Andrea Steiner, the new girl your agency just signed?"

"Yeah."

An image of the tall, lean blond rushed into Roxanne's mind. When Roxanne had first met the woman, she'd thought Andrea the quintessential All-American white girl with lovely pink skin and sparkling blue eyes. But when Roxanne had last seen Andrea, her skin had turned sallow. There'd been circles under her eyes and her soft curves had sharpened into angles. Even her smile had looked strained, painted on.

Roxanne was still a newcomer in fashion, but she'd been in the industry long enough to know what could cause such a sudden change—and it wasn't food poisoning.

The thought popped through her mind and passed her lips

before she could stop it. "I don't think food poisoning is responsible for how she looked when you guys left for Madrid."

Hunter's tone was tight, defensive. "What else would it be?"

"She looked sickly the last time I saw her, and not very happy," Roxanne said, choosing her words carefully. "I'm, I don't know, worried about her, I guess."

She could hear Hunter's eyes roll across the phone line. "Worried about her? You barely know her."

"True, but she's new. Modeling is hard. You have to be perfect all the time, which is impossible. Maybe she needs some help. *Divine* has excellent in-house counseling resources, and I'm sure Andrea would qualify since she does so much work for the magazine."

"Counseling?" Hunter repeated, his usually subtle accent clipping on the vowels. "What are you trying to say, Roxanne— you think she has an eating disorder or drug addiction or something?"

"I just know how hard your job is. How hard the industry, in general, can be, especially for women." An unexpected heat had crept into Roxanne's voice, and her fingers tightened around the steering wheel. "I just think it's important she knows there's resources available, that's all."

Hunter scoffed. "Come on, Roxanne, that's presumptuous. And potentially insulting."

"Wouldn't it be more insulting to not care about someone who might need help?" she shot back. "It's not like eating disorders are well-kept secrets in the fashion industry. Over 62% of models have been asked to lose weight or change their shape or size for the sake of their careers. Some people even call anorexia an occupational hazard."

Heavy silence suffocated the interior of the car, and Roxanne made a mental note to check in on Andrea after the holidays herself. Nothing was more disheartening than seeing women destroy themselves just because they didn't think they were beautiful enough. The criteria of what was considered beauty was one of the things she hoped to have an effect on in fashion, even if it didn't change the whole industry. After all, progress was paved in baby steps.

Besides, maybe Hunter was right and her hunch was wrong. Still, if she *was* right, the last thing she wanted was for Andrea to feel alone. She didn't have to be best friends with the woman to care about her health.

"Anyway, I don't think I'll be back for Christmas," Hunter continued when the silence remained unbroken. "If I'm lucky, we'll make it in before New Year. Sorry, babe."

He sounded courteous. Strained. Perhaps a little disappointed. Nervous, maybe, that she wouldn't take the news well. But he didn't sound *sorry*.

"Oh, that's too bad, but it's okay." Roxanne unfurled her fingers from the wheel and twiddled the air-conditioning presets, swallowing away the weird taste that had filled her mouth when Hunter called her *babe*. They were past pet names, weren't they? Roxanne assumed those had ended along with their relationship. Even so, at least now she didn't have to feel guilty about ditching him for the holidays at the last minute. "My family asked me to join them in Vermont to give my Grandma Myrtle a good last Christmas. At our family cabin—remember the one I told you about?"

There was another moment of silence on the other end of the line. Hunter made a sound halfway between clearing his throat and a cough. "Vermont?"

Roxanne turned the air conditioner all the way to high, then clicked it down to the off position. "Yes, Vermont. I am just about to head out of the City."

"Oh."

Hunter breathed across the line, obviously considering this new information. There was a time his deep rumble would have made her weak in the knees, but the effect had long since lost its potency. Now she waited impatiently for him to process and respond, like pushing a button on her lagging computer.

"Well, that'll be ... fun, right? Christmas in the Smokies, and all that?"

"Christmas in the *Green* Mountains," Roxanne corrected, feeling strangely proud of herself for knowing the difference. "But sure. Fun." She waited through another round of uncomfortable silence before adding, "I can text you the address, just in case."

"In case what?"

Implication clouded Hunter's voice, and Roxanne twisted another knob on the car's dashboard. "In case ... I don't know. Just in case."

"I could come up to Vermont, you know, when I get back. If you wanted."

The offer sounded less sincere than his version of an apology had. Roxanne clicked the air conditioner back on, then the heat. She knew she shouldn't be irked, but she was. Their last conversation had been a series of goodbyes—to Hunter as he departed for Madrid, to their topsy turvy relationship. Roxanne hadn't expected him to call, much less have any interest in spending the holidays with her, and the uneven temperature in the car was giving her vertigo. Why couldn't he have just wished her a good trip? He didn't have to play this game about meeting up later. They both knew he wouldn't come, even if she had invited him, which, technically, she hadn't.

Why had she even offered to send him the address? Did *she* want him to come?

Roxanne shook her head and forced herself to sound pleasant, smiling so the muscles of her throat would lift the tone of her voice, an old trick she'd learned in college public speaking classes. "Oh, no, you don't have to do that. I'll only be gone a few days."

"If you're sure …"

"I'm sure."

Hunter cleared his throat again. "Oh, hey, did you happen to hear back yet on any of those designs you submitted—the ones you sent up to Vivian?"

The knot in Roxanne's stomach melted into nausea. She checked to see if the driver's seat had a heating function. Of course, it did. "No. I haven't heard anything."

"And you gave her the good ones … the couture?"

"Yes." The word stuck on its way out. She'd wanted to show Vivian some of her more casual designs, fashions that would translate off the runway, but Hunter had convinced her to share her more daring designs instead—stuff she worried was a little out of her comfort zone, not to mention *actually* uncomfortable. She still wasn't sure it had been the right choice, but there was no sense in worrying about it now.

"Well, don't give up hope too soon. You know how slow

things can move in this business." Hunter paused. "And hey, when I get back … we should … we should talk about things, yeah? You know, really think about whether we have a future or not."

Or not. Roxanne twisted the air back to high. Of course, Hunter would drop a bomb like that when he was safely thousands of miles away on another continent. Drop it and hang up, leave her to squirm until he decided to come home. "Sure thing, yeah."

"Okay. Merry Christmas, babe." Hunter's voice sounded far away.

"Yep, you, too." She made the words as merry as she could manage. "Babe."

Not trusting her voice to speak again, Roxanne waited until there was static on the line before ending the call. When the low hum of the radio filled the space where Hunter's voice had been, she let out a deep breath, stretched her neck to pop out the tension, and shifted the car into drive.

She pointed the nose of her BMW toward the Green Mountains, all the while thinking about the mountain man Spencer had teased her about. Hey, why not?

Chapter Three

Once Roxanne had navigated through the congestion of the boroughs and made her way out of the heart of New York City, the highway northward opened up. She'd left work a few hours early to hit the road, but there weren't many cars on the road three days before Christmas Eve, even at rush hour. Perhaps most other holiday travelers heading into the mountains hadn't waited until the last minute and had already made their trek out of the City.

Or maybe the Vermont backwoods aren't a popular holiday destination and I'm the only one cabin-bound, Roxanne thought with a laugh. Doubling down on the lack of demand for her holiday destination was easier than believing she'd lucked into an easy commute only a few days before the biggest holiday of the year.

Nevertheless, once the sour taste the conversation with Hunter had left in her mouth had faded, the drive became noticeably more pleasant. Well, fine. No big deal, right? She'd already come to terms with this being their last turn on the on-again, off-again merry-go-round, and now she could ring in the New Year a single woman, ready for a fresh start. New year, new you and all that.

She turned up the radio. Few stations were playing anything other than seasonal tunes, and she let herself be swept away in holiday carols.

As Roxanne continued north, the trees became denser, and the black road gave way to pavement dusted with the slight silver sheen of fallen snow. Frost-covered evergreen trees lined both sides of the road and a light sprinkle of snowfall drifted downward from the sky. The view was no Rockefeller Center tree or Macy's light display, but it had a beauty of its own. *The sort that doesn't need a fancy brand name,* she considered.

Roxanne stopped once for gas and coffee in Albany, shivering inside her expensive fleece-lined jacket. Otherwise, the drive was uneventful. Quiet. Peaceful, even.

Quaint, she thought, somewhat ruefully. Roxanne had forgotten the type of silence that came from being truly away from Manhattan. It wasn't so much a lack of noise as a calmness that settled over everything and wrapped itself around her like a warm, comforting blanket.

Quaint. Although still a little sharp around the edges, the word didn't sound quite so bad a second time around. Roxanne turned down the radio and listened to the sound of her own breathing. Was this what quiet sounded like—peace on Earth? It had been so long since Roxanne had heard it, she couldn't be sure. She loved the City but had become unfamiliar with what it felt like to be away from it—not the city proper, but New York City as a *thing* in itself. She couldn't remember the last time she had felt this stillness. There were no impatient taxis, no speed-walking pedestrians, no buildings or signs or other evidence of humanity obstructing her view of the natural world. Every once in a while, she'd pass a lone diner or a sign would pop up announcing a turnoff, but otherwise Roxanne was completely alone—just her, the car, and the open road.

"If it weren't so quaint, it might actually be a nice drive," she muttered aloud to the empty car. "Like a spa day, with stale gas station coffee instead of cucumber water, but not half bad." She considered the thin cardboard cup of coffee she'd picked up at the gas station, tipped it in mock salute to the open road, and took a sip as she watched the snow-covered landscape pass by. "Not bad at all."

A rendition of "Do They Know It's Christmas" came on the radio and Roxanne thumbed up the volume.

She could forget finding someone serving decent coffee in these parts, but she could manage without it. More concerning was how she was going to survive her actual family. They would inevitably be full of nosy questions and snide remarks about her lifestyle, of that she was certain. Roxanne's parents had never been big fans of her career choice in the fashion industry and had urged her to settle down with someone more down to earth. What would they say if she told them she'd shared some of her designs with her boss? Her mom and dad would likely smile and nod agreeably, say something about hard work. Rachel would probably ask questions Roxanne wasn't prepared to answer—like why Hunter hadn't come with her.

But not Grandma Myrtle. Grandma Myrtle would be excited and would ask to see the designs. Grandma Myrtle was the only one who had ever truly believed in Roxanne's dreams, or her ability to reach them. She'd been the reason Roxanne had left home and gone to design school in the first place.

Grandma Myrtle was also the main reason Roxanne was out alone, driving uphill through frost-covered forest, to spend Christmas in the woods. *It's only a few days*, she told herself. Only a few days and then she'd be back to civilization, as Spencer had called it.

Roxanne set the cruise control on her steering wheel and let her body melt into the car's heated seat. She rolled her neck, enjoying the sensation of the pressure giving way as the tension she'd been carrying cracked and loosened. She let her thoughts wander as the sky faded from blue to purple, deepening steadily into twilight, and the snow continued to fall as she sped farther into the snow mountains, humming along to the low sounds of radio carols.

An hour later, the radio station she'd been listening to crinkled to static, and Roxanne pressed the button on the steering wheel to search for an available broadcasting channel. The first recognizable sounds she heard were the notes of a carol she'd heard a dozen times already. She grimaced and pushed the button again.

"Blizzard inbound." On the next station, a brief series of alert chimes heralded the self-important voice of a radio DJ cutting through the last few notes of a familiar melody.

The DJ continued his warning, listing off names of towns and landmarks Roxanne had never heard of as he prattled on about road conditions and impending weather with an unnecessary amount of cheer. She paid it no attention at first, until she realized she was, in fact, driving the very roads being described. She nudged up the volume.

"—so stay off the roads tonight if you can, folks," the DJ was saying. "If you've gotta be out, don't forget your tire chains and flares and make sure you're bundled up. It's gonna be whiteout conditions before you know it, and with the holidays coming, I'm afraid Santa and his flying reindeer will be the only ones getting out and about for the next couple of days."

Crap. Roxanne hadn't considered how things like weather might affect her drive. What exactly were tire chains, anyway? She certainly didn't own any, much less have them with her. She couldn't have stopped somewhere to sort it all out now anyway.

"Well, that's just fantastic." Roxanne eyed the roadside trees that had turned into white cones under a heavy blanket of snow. The light flurry of snowfall had thickened into a deluge of frost and ice while she'd been lost in her thoughts, and idyllic greeting card landscape before her now appeared severe and dangerous. Frozen. Roxanne turned on the defroster and gripped the steering wheel, inadvertently pressing the volume button with her palm. The radio's volume shot up again, shattering what was left of her dabbles with inner peace.

"One more time for those listeners just tuning in," the announcer boomed, his polished radio vibrato hammering through the speakers on the now too-loud stereo. "We're expecting at least a good eighteen inches tonight, more in the mountain areas, and it won't be stopping anytime soon. Expect roads to be closed north of Burlington and forget the mountain passes. Buckle in, folks. It's going to be a very cold and a very white Christmas. Ho ho ho!"

The tight feeling in her neck had returned, and by the time the DJ's voice had been replaced by a new tune—"Winter Wonderland"—the snow was coming down so heavily she could barely see the front of her car's hood. Visibility was pretty much nonexistent. She slowed to a crawl and flipped the windshield wipers as fast as they would go. The defroster was on full blast and barely making a dent in the frost accumulation. Her all-season tires slipped on the ice.

Roxanne checked the in-dash navigation screen. She was less than twenty miles from the turnoff to her family's cabin. Twenty miles, she could make that. She could even call for help, ask her dad to come out in the truck and guide her in. For a moment Roxanne felt a sweet rush of relief, but then she checked her phone. No signal ... and her battery was almost dead.

Double fantastic. She'd been so distracted after the call with Hunter she'd forgotten to plug the phone into the charger—not that it would do her a lot of good without cell service.

Roxanne gritted her teeth, wishing she had laser vision to cut through the sheet of white in front of her. If she could make it a few more miles, she'd be there. If not, well, she just hoped one of the two people she'd told where she was going would think to check on her and report her missing at some point before her body froze over in the Vermont tundra. Of course, Hunter was in Europe and Spencer expected her to be out of touch anyway. Her parents would assume she'd ghosted them, which would be believable enough, considering she'd already pushed her arrival to the last possible minute.

Perfect.

The snow kept falling faster and thicker, and the BMW's slick city tires were having a hard time maintaining their grip on the icy road. The car's speedometer had fallen nearly all the way to zero, but still the vehicle inched forward, and the defroster was keeping the windshield clear enough she could see the road ahead. Barely.

"Get off the road folks—"

"I've heard enough out of you," Roxanne snapped as the DJ launched into yet another warning. She unclenched one of her hands from the wheel and took her eyes off the road for just a second, intending to shut off the radio.

A dark blur sped in front of the car. She didn't get a clear view—it might have been a lump of falling snow or it could have been an animal—but Roxanne started, stomped her foot on the brake … and felt the car give way beneath her.

She spun once, twice, three times, before the car came to a sudden, abrupt stop. The inertia caused her head to smack against the window, a curious sound of sleigh bells jingled in her ears, and then everything white faded to black.

Chapter Four

Roxanne opened her eyes to a small pinpoint of bright light glaring into her vision. For a moment she had the odd sensation of feeling warm and weightless, like she was floating in a pool of bathwater, or relaxing in the sauna at her favorite spa in the City, but the feeling of warm serenity faded as her senses returned. She found herself bundled in a thick woolen blanket and settled against a bank of soft snow.

And it was cold. Freezing.

Blinking, she could make out flakes still falling, billowing in huge flurries under the moonlight. The red glow of her car's taillights flashed around her, casting odd, pink-tinted punctuations on the white. The driver's side door of her car was hanging wide open a few yards away. Roxanne could still hear the radio jockey's voice warning about bad weather and poor road conditions, chastising anyone—who, like her—had been silly enough to be traveling on a night like tonight. Roxanne's head pounded too hard to bother trying to make out anything beyond that. What was the verbal command to turn off the radio? Maybe she could yell loud enough for the car to hear her, assuming she could remember what to tell it to do. *Shut up?* No, that probably wasn't it.

The flashing of the car's taillights seemed to thrum in Roxanne's ears. The pinpoint of light danced in front of her. She could still hear the DJ talking, but his voice was muffled. What was he saying? Something about a freak blizzard, and—

Through the hazy din in her head, Roxanne became aware a man was leaning over her, trying to get her attention as he tested her pupils with a penlight. He was wearing a full wardrobe of heavy winter gear, his features largely obscured beneath a knit cap, scarf, and the high collar of a down ski coat. A pair of deep-set eyes peered down at her, and she could see the high bridge of a Grecian nose exposed in the space between the layers of his winter gear.

Is he the DJ? No, that couldn't be right.

"Can you hear me?" A voice spoke somewhere far away, muffled and fuzzy like it was coming through an underground tunnel. Or maybe it was above her. "Can you hear me?"

Loud. The sound boomed around Roxanne's head. She groaned and struggled to cover her ears. The ground spun beneath her and then lurched to a stop. She heaved, tasting old coffee.

"Hey, you're all right. Can you hear me?"

Above her, the man removed the penlight and held it pointed down, so the beam cast a bright halo off the snow. Roxanne blinked away the circle of shadow left in her vision, and the world seemed to finally settle back into place. She furrowed her brows and shook her head, meeting the worried gaze of the man above her. Without the glare in her eyes, Roxanne could see his eyes were dark green, pine and ivy, and they were framed by a pair of dark eyebrows currently arched in concern.

"What's your name?"

"Roxanne." Her voice sounded hollow, lazy. It felt weird to say her own name—her lips struggled to shape the words, and her throat was scratchy. She tried to sit up, but the snow swirled faster, and she lay back against the bank as the ground seemed to give way beneath her again. Clearly, she'd been in a car accident. That must have been what had happened—right? All she could remember was a dark blur streaking across her windshield and the jingling sound of sleigh bells. The last part must have been her imagination. There hadn't been any music playing on the radio, just the DJ and his obnoxious warnings.

"Roxanne Hudson." This time the words felt more normal when they fell out of her mouth, and the thoughts swirling in her mind tumbled between her lips. "Did I hit something? I think I hit a deer. Or something bigger than a deer." She pulled her arms loose of the blanket bundle and pressed her fingers against her temples. "I heard bells."

The light flashed in her eyes, blinding her again. Delicate snowflakes muddled together and thudded to the ground in thick clumps of white.

"Don't see anything hit, other than your car," the man answered. "You must have gotten spooked, hit the brakes, and spun out into the snow. Good thing you were driving slowly. Those tires aren't made for driving in conditions like this, you know—aren't even chains on 'em. Lucky for you the snow is still soft, hasn't had time to pack up and harden. Otherwise, you would have spun into a solid wall of ice, and I doubt we'd be having this conversation right now."

The penlight shifted from one eye to the other, its beam wavering in the snowy wind between them. "Can't get a good look at your pupils. You may have a concussion."

Roxanne grunted softly and kept her hand pressed to her head. "Right."

There was a click as the man switched off the penlight, then the crunch of snow as he lowered to a squat beside her. A rush of scents came with him—pepper, earthy vetiver, and vanilla with a creamy finish of notes of cardamom and cinnamon.

Smells like Christmas. Roxanne tried to push the thought out of her head, but the motion made her dizzy all over again.

The man raised a gloved hand to his face and tugged the neck gaiter down under his chin, revealing an angular jaw. A swatch of dark brown beard dotted with snowflakes framed a wide mouth, and when he spoke, his teeth were nearly the same shade of white as the snow. "You said your name was Hudson," he repeated. "Any relation to Robert Hudson, keeps a cabin up on Cranberry Hill? Used to belong to old Jimmy Hudson before he passed a few years back."

Roxanne nodded, or tried to. The movement was cut short when her stomach churned and her vision swam. "Jimmy Hudson is my grandfather. Or, he was." She paused to breathe. "Robert Hudson is my father. I'm on my way to the cabin. We're spending Christmas there."

She felt like she was rambling, but the shock of her accident had worn off and the reality of her current situation was setting in. Panic overtook the thumping in her head, and she propelled herself upward, looking from the hood of her BMW halfway buried in a bank of snow several feet away to the hulking man squatting within arm's length of her. The falling snow had already almost buried her car in white.

Who was this man and how had he found her? So far, he'd done nothing but make sure she was unharmed, but being stranded in the middle of nowhere in a snowstorm with a strange man was the sort of thing that would get you killed in New York, and she didn't want to play the odds. Nothing good ever came out of a situation like that, even if it was the most wonderful time of the year. Peace on Earth, goodwill to men, and so forth—you didn't see a lot of that in the headlines.

"Easy, easy," the man coaxed, his palms patting at the air between them. He had to raise his voice to be heard over the wind. "You don't want to move around too quick until we make sure you're okay."

Adrenaline rushed through Roxanne. She scrambled to her feet despite his warning and the pain in her head, throwing the blanket to the ground and holding her hands out in front of her as she inched backward toward the car. There was a can of mace in her purse, and maybe she could manage a bar of cell signal to call her family—let them know where she was, so they could send help or come pick her up. Maybe this helpful Samaritan would be less likely to try any funny business if he knew her father and brother-in-law were on their way.

"They're waiting on me, you know," she warned, still backing away until the heels of her boots stopped against the edge of her car. Her eyes darted to the clock on the dashboard, and Roxanne discovered she'd lost an hour. It was full dark out now, well past dinnertime. What in the winter wonderland had she hit? "I should have been there already, actually. They're probably already looking for me."

She felt around behind her for her purse. Finding it, she

slipped her hand into its interior pocket, curling her fingers reassuringly around the small mace can. Roxanne loosed a sigh of relief and hoped it wasn't audible. What kind of reaction would Spencer have if she told him she'd wrecked her car on the drive to Vermont and found herself going head-to-head with some random mountain man? Maybe she wouldn't tell him.

The stranger pulled his neck gaiter farther down his neck until it bundled with his scarf. With everything below his eyebrows exposed, Roxanne had a full view of his face, but the two were separated by several feet of night, and so she didn't see much more now than she had before—just the glimmer of eyeshine in the blinking flash of her taillights. He took a step forward, pushing one gloved hand slowly into his pocket while the other splayed palm-first toward Roxanne as if she were a frightened animal.

"I don't mean you any harm. I'm a ranger." He withdrew his arm from his coat and slowly extended his hand to her.

Clutched in his glove was a bifold wallet, held open in the center to reveal two official-looking documents. A shiny, legitimate-looking badge was on one side—the kind normally worn pinned to a uniform. The words *Green Mountain Patrol* were engraved on the badge's top. On the opposite side of the wallet was a laminated ID card with his name and photograph, taken from the shoulders up, and other details of his position too small to read in the dim light.

"My name is Mark, Mark Foster."

Roxanne snatched the wallet from the ranger's hand and, angling her body between the man and the car, studied the photograph under the light of her open door. The man standing in front of her in the snow had his hair hidden beneath a beanie, but in the photograph it was coal-black, combed over neatly to the side in one of those evergreen men's fashions that stayed in style regardless of the decade. Wide red lips curved into an easy, friendly sort of disarming smile, and his beard was trimmed enough not to mask the strong angle of his cheekbones, or to disguise the sharp curve of his jaw. She recognized his eyes—large and kind above a long, narrow nose.

Mark the Ranger had a photographic quality too warm to be caught on camera and too rare to be found in most men Roxanne had encountered, especially in the types she knew in New York. She extended her arm to return the wallet.

"Seems official," she offered, attempting to sound like she'd never been concerned he wasn't.

Mark took the proffered wallet and tucked it back into his coat with a small smile.

"Glad you think so. Now, Roxanne Hudson, let's see about getting you out of the snow and home in time for Christmas."

Chapter Five

Given her rescuer was indeed an actual, bona fide rescuer, Roxanne had assumed Mark Foster would have had an official vehicle waiting somewhere just out of sight, or some other form of automotive salvation. A snowmobile, or even a sleigh. Unfortunately, she discovered this was not the case.

"So, do you, like, have a patrol truck or something?" she asked, craning her head around him as if one might magically appear in the darkness beyond the blinking tail lights of her useless car. The snow was coming down in a solid sheet of white now, and she held her forearm up to her forehead to keep the stuff from getting in her eyes.

"No ma'am," Mark replied with a sheepish sort of smirk. Snowflakes decorated his eyebrows, and the bits of beard peeking out above his downturned gaiter sparkled like glitter in the dark. "I was out for a hike when I came across you here. Wasn't expecting to find anyone out in these conditions."

The ranger's excuse for being out in this weather sounded crazier than Roxanne's holiday-bound blizzard commute. "A hike?" she echoed incredulously, then gestured around as much as she could with stiff, frozen arms. "You mean you were willingly out walking around in this?"

He shrugged.

"Some of us like the snow. Besides, my place is right up there"—he pointed at the dark forest—"less than a quarter of a mile. If I hadn't stumbled across you, I would have been home before it got too bad out. Doesn't matter now. I know the path like the back of my hand. We can make it easily."

"How easily?" Roxanne couldn't help but notice she'd lost feeling in her toes.

"With any luck, we'll take the snowcat back down to get your things and have you up to your family's cabin in an hour, maybe two if visibility gets any worse. Landlines are probably down, but we can use the radio to let your folks know you're all right. I'm sure Robert has it on."

Snowcat? Roxanne wasn't sure what a snowcat was, but she was familiar with the cabin's radio. It was basically a piece of furniture, an antique ham radio formerly belonging to her Grandpa Jimmy. She remembered playing on the old radio with her grandfather when she'd been a girl, but she'd never used it herself. Like his father before him, Roxanne's dad was a fan of broadcast; he'd definitely have the radio on, especially if it was the only source of incoming news. She nodded in agreement and didn't ask what the snowcat might be, figuring she'd know it when she saw it. As long as it wasn't some sort of *actual* animal, she'd be fine.

The snow was coming down heavier now, if such a thing was possible, the whiteout so bright it was almost blinding. Roxanne had heard of, but never seen, whiteout conditions, but assumed

37

this situation qualified. Mark stepped in closer, otherwise, the snowfall was so dense he might have been eclipsed from her view from only a few feet away.

"We need to get moving, then. I'm freezing." Roxanne had to raise her voice to make sure she was heard above a sudden gust of icy wind. She hugged her arms around herself, balling her hands into fists and rubbing them furiously on her arms for friction. The fleece-lined jacket was useless in this kind of cold, and the frosty wind bit at her through the fabric, nipping and stinging her skin despite her best efforts to cultivate some body heat. The beanie she'd brought just for the trip was likewise inefficient when she pulled it from her bag and pushed it down over her hair. The frozen air sliced through the knitting, and she had nothing to warm her hands—or pockets to stuff them in. Why did women's clothes never come with enough pockets?

The hair under the cap became wet and rigid with cold, and her fingers ached. Roxanne felt like the little girl, Karen, in *Frosty the Snowman*, at the moment she nearly froze to death on her quest to return the snowman home to the North Pole. Santa himself had saved them both, and she hoped Mark the Ranger, in his thick winter wear, would be just as capable. "I don't think I've ever been this cold in my life."

Mark had returned the neck gaiter over his mouth, but Roxanne could still see the way he was looking at her—like she'd said something silly but he was too polite to remark on it.

"Is this the warmest coat you have?" he asked, pulling the gaiter away from his lips. His eyebrows knitted in concern.

She shivered in response.

"What other gear do you have? We need to get you warmed

up before the cold gets in your bones."

"I have another coat in the trunk."

The ranger motioned to the car's back end and Roxanne hit the button on the BMW's console to pop it open. As Mark rummaged, Roxanne slid into the driver's seat and killed the engine, then grabbed her purse, stepped out of the car, and shut the door behind her. She hit the automatic lock button on her key fob and tucked it into her purse as Mark lifted her winter coat out of the trunk.

"Is this it?" He held up her green winter parka by its removable faux fur hood. He didn't seem impressed.

"Yes."

Roxanne reached for the jacket, but Mark gave the parka an appraising look and tossed it back into the trunk without handing it over.

"You forgot to give me the coat," Roxanne snapped, stuffing her stiff frozen fingers into her purse to fish out her fob and reopen the trunk.

"That coat is as useless as the one you're wearing."

"What are you talking about?" Roxanne stared, dumfounded. "Just so you know, *that* coat has been a best-selling style for over thirty years. I even had it altered." She recited the line the clerk at the department store had given her when she'd bought it as a last-minute decision, more impressed by the slim fit and tapered waistline than its winter qualifications, which had been listed on a tag she hadn't bothered to read. The parka wasn't fashionable enough to be her first choice, or her third, but then again, she hadn't expected to spend more time in the snow than the walk from her car to the cabin, so it hadn't really mattered.

Mark shrugged. "Well, that may be so, but it still won't do much for you in this kind of cold. You'll be warmer in the fleece. Even in layers, the down would just trap the cold air against you without anything to wick away your skin's moisture. You can get hypothermia without being wet, you know."

Mark moved toward her, his boots crunching in the snow as he walked. Roxanne was still rummaging for her keys, cursing the ranger under her breath, but her hands were so cold her fingers didn't seem to be working, and she could barely feel the items in her purse. So what if the coat wasn't up to his standards? She was freezing and anything had to be better than the Sherpa-lined disappointment she was wearing.

The cold was making her grumpy. Her head was also still pounding, and the snowflakes were beginning to blur into wispy white smears again. She was having a hard time keeping track of how close Mark was to her—he seemed close, then farther away, then closer than before. Every time his distance changed the sound of sleigh bells was in her ears again. The bright white of the snowfall faded to gray, and even though she was shivering she didn't feel cold anymore.

Before Roxanne realized it was happening, she was falling, but no sooner had she discovered this than she was also aware of Mark's arms around her, holding her upright against his chest. He was warm, simultaneously hard and soft, and solid beneath the puffy thickness of his coat. Roxanne stared up into his brilliant green eyes and her feet turned liquid. He looked down at her and said something reassuring about getting her in from the cold, then Roxanne closed her eyes and let herself go limp in the ranger's arms.

Chapter Six

When Roxanne opened her eyes, she was out of the cold, snowy darkness and lying on the well-worn cushions of an overstuffed couch, covered in layers of warm blankets. Her feet felt awkward and heavy, and she pushed them out from underneath the blanket to discover her boots had been removed and replaced by a thick pair of woolen socks and too-large men's house slippers. Her own shoes, as well as her purse, rested across the armrest at the far end of the couch.

Roxanne scanned the room, taking in its creature comforts and minimalism. A fire was roaring from within the belly of a deep stone fireplace, adding to the low lamplight, and a large golden retriever was asleep on the floor between Roxanne's couch and the hearth. The room smelled strongly of cinnamon and coffee. There was a large, undecorated fir tree in the corner, crowded by a few nicely wrapped gifts, but otherwise the room was spare of holiday decorations. Beside the tree sat a box brimming with garland and several boxes of what looked like unwrapped packages. One stocking hung on the mantel, held in place with a bottle of bourbon. A large rawhide bone poked out of its top.

"Is that for you?" she asked the dog. It thumped its tail happily in response.

Roxanne pulled herself upright and wound her legs underneath her as she settled more comfortably on the couch. Aside from the dog, she was alone in the room, which appeared to be the den of a rustic cabin, though it looked more like a home than a vacation spot. Furthermore, it was clearly a bachelor pad. What looked like the entire contents of a sport equipment store lined around the room's edges, but the space was tidy and well appointed. In addition to the various bits of outdoorsy gear, there were several bookshelves crammed full of various books and stacks of papers. An old-fashioned turntable sat in one corner, accompanied by several wooden crates filled with 45s, and an antique grandfather clock ticked out the time. It wasn't fancy, but it was comfortable.

"Glad to see you're awake."

Behind her, Ranger Mark Foster passed through an open doorway to Roxanne's left, two steaming, mismatched mugs gripped in his hands. He had rid himself of the bulky winter gear, and Roxanne tried not to stare. The photograph on his ranger ID had not done him justice.

"Was I out a long time?"

"A little while. Not too long."

"Oh. Good." The static picture hadn't shown how his thin cotton tee clung to taut muscles as he moved, or the smooth, molten way he walked. How the ropey veins in his hand twisted as he sat one of the mugs on the coffee table in front of her. The earthy scent of musk and vanilla she'd noticed before still clung to his skin. Heat radiated off his body and buffeted against hers as he passed by inches from her.

"How are you feeling?" Mark asked, lowering himself into a faded blue armchair at the other end of the couch.

"Not bad, I guess. My head is still kind of fuzzy."

"It'll clear up. Don't worry."

Roxanne tried to ignore the way Mark's green eyes gleamed in the firelight, and the dimple that appeared in his cheek when he lifted the mug and blew away the steam before taking a sip.

"Is this your place?" Roxanne closed her eyes and shook her head. Of course, it was his place. He'd said his cabin was close by, hadn't he? "How did I get here? The last thing I remember ..." A series of faint images came to her—her car in the snow, dizzying white flooding from the sky, the sound of bells, Mark's arms around her, and darkness. She shook her head, trying to rattle the pieces into a cohesive whole. "I must have hit my head harder than I thought."

"You did." Mark's smile was patient. "I ran a concussion protocol when I found you. Do you remember that?"

"I remember you shining a light in my eyes."

He nodded. "I was checking your pupils. You hit your head, but other than a bad headache and a little overall wooziness, you'll be right as rain in no time. Just need to process the shock of the whole thing, and nothing helps more than a little rest."

"I don't remember the walk to your ..." Roxanne looked around, searching for the correct word, and reached for the mug. The scent of cider, thick and spicy, met her as she lifted it to her lips. "Your house. How did we get here?"

The low light in the room made it hard to be sure, but it looked like Mark had turned pink underneath his coffee-brown

43

beard. "I carried you."

The cider slid down Roxanne's throat too quickly, and she coughed to clear her throat. Her legs had gone numb. Was she experiencing awe or embarrassment or both—something else?

"You *carried* me?"

Mark leaned forward so his elbows rested on the tops of his knees, then took a sip from his mug. "I couldn't leave you in the snow. Luckily for me, you're an easy carry." He winked at her over the edge of his cider and nodded in the direction of the retriever still sleeping by the fire. "I've had rougher treks lugging the ol' man around."

Roxanne looked to the dog. Its golden fur was tipped in gray. "What's his name?"

"Bogart."

The dog thumped his tail on the wooden floor at hearing his name, and he peeled open eyes as golden as his coat and focused them on his owner.

Mark leaned forward to rumple the dog's fur. "Named after one of history's greatest actors."

"Oh." Roxanne's surprise at the dog's name shot out of her mouth. "That's …" She let her voice trail off, realizing what she'd almost said might have been rude.

Mark cocked a curious eyebrow at her, and so did Bogart. The dog pushed himself from the floor, a movement which appeared to require a considerable amount of effort, and made his way sluggishly to Mark, where he nuzzled against his owner's empty hand, hoping to be petted.

"That's what?" Mark asked, stroking the dog's ear.

Roxanne shrugged, embarrassed. "It's just awfully

sophisticated for a ... well ..." The words were even more incriminating out loud, and they stuck unsaid in her throat.

"For a rough old mountain man's dog?" Mark finished for her and laughed. "Yeah, I guess so, huh?"

He laughed again, and Roxanne let out a sigh of relief. *The guy rescues you out of a car wreck in a blizzard, and the first thing you do is insult his dog's name.*

"Call him Bogie most of the time, though," Mark said. "He seems to prefer it anyway."

"Bogie," Roxanne echoed, and the dog lifted his head from Mark's lap and fixed his liquid copper eyes on her. She smiled at him. "He looks sweet."

"Ah, he's all right," Mark joked, patting Bogie's head. "Go on and lay back down, old man." He nudged the dog back toward his resting place by the fire. "Rest those bones, boy. It's almost Christmastime."

Almost Christmastime. The word spurred Roxanne's thoughts to action. She jerked, nearly spilling the hot cider into her lap. "My parents—I need to update them. It must be late. Can I use your radio?"

"You think they'll still be up?" Mark's eyes swept to the grandfather clock. "It's past midnight. I thought about radioing in when we got back, but I wanted to wait until you woke up so you could talk yourself."

Roxanne bit back a laugh. The holidays were a twenty-four hour a day event with her family, the hour of the day less important than the time spent with loved ones. One of Roxanne's most cherished childhood memories was an all-night baking spree with her mom, sister, and Grandma Myrtle. They'd mixed, baked, and decorated Christmas cookies all night, and when the sun had come up, they'd dined on gingerbread men for breakfast. It wasn't one of the healthiest meals she'd ever had, but certainly one of the happiest.

"They'll be up," she said.

Mark set his mug on the coffee table. "Then let's do it. The radio is in the kitchen." He stood and extended his hand. "You might be a little shaky on your feet for a while still. Let me help you."

Roxanne swung her legs out and tried to stand but found Mark's supposition to be accurate. The wooden floor was unsteady, and the movement made her dizzy, like she was trying to find her balance on the swaying deck of a sailboat. She'd intended to prove she could stand on her own, but she accepted Mark's hand and pushed herself up. Seconds later, Roxanne found herself holding onto the ranger's thick forearms for dear life as the floor tilted unexpectedly beneath her.

"Oh my god. I seriously underestimated my ability to stand. I'm so sorry." Roxanne's cheeks warmed as she allowed herself to rest inside the circle of Mark's arms, her feet struggling to find solid ground.

Mark chuckled as he squared his body behind hers so he could support her weight. They moved together toward the kitchen. "I hate to say I told you so, but I'm here to help. One step at a time."

Roxanne readied herself to be offended, but she wasn't. Much to her surprise, she laughed back. Had it been anyone else wrapped around her, she'd have been humiliated. Somehow, she didn't mind it so much in Mark's arms. Actually, it felt kind of wonderful.

Like the den, the kitchen was minimal, masculine, and surprisingly modest. A large farm table took up most of the room, and a variety of well-seasoned cast iron pans were hung on the wall above a wide kitchen window that was home to an assortment of small pots filled with herbs. The sink was empty, but the scent of recently cooked food hung in the air. Her stomach clenched. She'd missed dinner, but until now hadn't even realized she was hungry.

Three days till Christmas was shortening quickly to two.

Mark guided her to the radio in the corner of the kitchen. He pulled a chair from the farm table and helped her into it before he turned his attention to the radio, twisting and turning knobs and dials. Static crinkled in the air before softening into white noise. There was a small notebook lying next to the radio and Roxanne watched Mark pick it up and thumb through several pages before landing on Hudson, R. A random jumble of letters accompanied the names on Mark's list.

"Have you ever used a ham radio before?" he asked, holding the microphone out to her.

She had to laugh. "I have not. I haven't even used in a landline in longer than I can remember, much less a phone as big as a piece of furniture. I wouldn't even know what a ham radio was if my grandfather hadn't kept one in our cabin."

"What, you mean to tell me this isn't standard equipment where you live?" Mark's tone was teasing. "And here I thought I had the latest and greatest in communication technology."

"Not since at least the 1920s." Roxanne wasn't exactly sure

when ham radios had enjoyed their prime.

Mark twisted another knob and something beeped. "Fair enough. Cell phone's probably more convenient."

"Definitely easier to carry in one's pocket."

He chuckled his agreement. "Well, the ham radio's not fancy, but there's not much to it. You'll hold this when you talk"—Mark used his thumb to press a small button on the side of the receiver— "and release it when you're listening. I know your father's call sign, so if you don't mind, I'll get him on and hand it over. Sound good?"

"Sounds good to me." Roxanne was relieved all she had to do was push a button and talk—she didn't even know what a call sign was.

Mark nodded and fussed with another knob on the radio, then cleared his throat. "This is CQ TB1NRK. Tango Bravo One November Romeo Kilo. TB1NRK calling CQ FK1WTB. Foxtrot Kilo One Whiskey Tango Bravo. Standing by for a call."

Mark's overly formal radio voice made Roxanne's knees weak in a way that had nothing to do with the shock from her car accident. She crossed her legs and tried to look composed.

Static buzzed again, and within moments, a familiar voice came through the speaker. "CQ TB1NRK Tango Bravo One November Romeo Kilo. This is CQ FK1WTB Foxtrot Kilo One Whiskey Tango Bravo. Line open. Switching to private frequency. Over."

Mark pushed a button on the radio and started speaking in his own voice again. "Hello Robert, this is Mark Foster with the Green Mountain Patrol. I've got your daughter, Roxanne, here—she's been in a mild accident, but she's safe. Handing over to Roxanne now. Over."

He released the talk button and waited. "10-4," came Robert Hudson's voice.

Mark handed Roxanne the radio, showing her where to press as her father's voice came through the speaker again.

"Hi Dad, it's me."

"Say 'over' when you're done, then depress the mic button," Mark instructed in a whisper, using his hands to help her fingers feel the buttons.

Roxanne's skin turned warm where he'd touched it. "Over," she said and let go of the button. Mark gave her a thumbs up and moved away to give her a measure of privacy.

"Roxy, are you all right, honey?" Her father sounded worried. "We've been wondering where you were. Couldn't get you on your cell. Thought you might have turned back. What happened? Over."

Roxanne pressed the switch and tried not to feel awkward speaking in front of Mark the Ranger. "I had some trouble in the snow and lost control of my car. But I'm fine, really. I'm at—she looked at Mark. "Well, I'm at Ranger Foster's cabin now," she said, unsure of how to address him. "But don't worry. I'll be there soon. He's going to bring me over in the snow cat mobile." She knew she got the last part wrong but couldn't remember exactly what Mark had called the thing and her head hurt too badly to think about it. She tossed her hair back, feigning confidence. He didn't correct her.

"Over," she added, almost forgetting.

Robert Hudson's voice was very fatherly when he spoke again. "Not at this hour, honey. Visibility is darn near zero. Don't want you to attempt it, not even with Ranger Foster, and he's probably the best snowcatter in these parts. Stay put tonight, kiddo, and have Foster bring you out tomorrow. Over."

Roxanne gaped. Did her dad seriously just tell her to stay the night in a strange man's cabin? She opened her mouth to argue but her father beat her to it.

"Hold on a minute, Roxy. Your Grandma Myrtle wants to speak with you."

A few beats later, her grandmother's voice warbled across the line. Roxanne hadn't spoken to Grandma Myrtle in years, too absorbed in her rising career to remember to keep in touch, but hearing it now flooded her with memories of Christmases past. An unexpected sadness welled in Roxanne's chest. It must have been the shock from her accident. Either that or her conscience was reminding her she'd been wrong not to call more often.

Grandma Myrtle's voice had thickened with age, but it came clearly across the radio. "Roxy, honey, are you there? Over."

"I'm here, Grandma. Over."

"Now, you do as your daddy says, honey. Stay safe and warm inside, and we'll see you tomorrow, you hear? Don't you worry about a thing. Over."

"I'm sorry I'm late, Grandma. I know how important it is to you we're all together for Christmas. Over."

Static crinkled on the radio before Myrtle came on again. "Oh, don't worry about that. We'll be here when you get here. Handing back to your dad now. Over."

Mark gestured for the receiver, and Roxanne handed it over, not sure what to say. He leaned to glance out the kitchen window at the weather and resumed his radio voice. "Robert, Mark Foster here. All confirmed. Looks like a whiteout. I'm happy to have Roxanne stay for the night. We'll head your way in the morning, assuming it's all clear. Over."

He held out the radio for Roxanne, but she shook her head. There wasn't anything else to say. It sounded like she was spending the night with the ranger whether she liked it or not.

"All good," Robert Hudson confirmed. "Take care of my little girl, Ranger. Over."

"I'll do my best, sir. Will leave the channel open. Over and out."

Mark busied himself turning knobs on the radio before facing Roxanne again. "Looks like we're in for the night."

Roxanne noticed a strain in Mark's voice for the first time. He wiped at his nose, and she thought she spied some redness on his face that hadn't been there before—not since the blush when he'd said he carried her home.

"Looks like it." There was a ripple in her own voice, too. "I hope it's okay."

"It's my pleasure. It's nice to have someone here." Mark smiled and extended his hand again.

This time, Roxanne accepted it without hesitating and allowed herself to be lifted from the kitchen chair. Still unsteady on her feet, she was grateful for his arm around her waist as he guided her back toward the den and the safe anchor of the sofa. Their eyes met as Mark lowered her onto the cushion, and Roxanne heard the jingle of sleigh bells again. Was that a normal aftereffect of her concussion? She'd have to remember to ask some other time when Mark's arms weren't around her.

She was officially snowed in with a handsome stranger. Christmas was turning out to be quite different than she'd expected.

Chapter Seven

After it was decided she was staying, Roxanne insisted on freshening up, then realized with horror none of her belongings—other than her purse and her dead cell phone—had made it to the cabin with her. Her luggage, including all of her clean clothes and toiletries, had been left behind, locked in the trunk of her snowbound BMW.

"All of my stuff is back in my car," she said, trying not to sound as panicked as she felt. "I don't have any clean clothes or other …" She trailed off as she ran her hands along the sweater and leggings. How wrinkled and filthy was she? She tried not to think about how mussed her hair must have been, or how faded her expertly applied makeup. At the very least, she was stale and wouldn't be caught dead in a photo in her current condition, blizzard or not.

For the first time since she'd woken up, Roxanne felt gritty and uncomfortable, simultaneously wanting to look into a mirror and horrified by the idea of seeing her reflection. Being stuck in yesterday's clothes—and showing up to face her family unshowered and wearing a two-day-old road-trip outfit—filled her with dread.

Mark gave her an apologetic look. "I didn't have enough arms for you and your suitcase."

Guilt surged and Roxanne dropped her head to avoid eye contact. "I'm so sorry. I didn't mean to sound ungrateful. It's not that at all." She'd rather be warm and dirty than clean and frozen. She just preferred to be cute, too.

He seemed to understand. "We can go back for your things first thing in the morning. We'll grab it and you can come back here and freshen up before we head over to your folks. I'll take a look at your car while we're there, too, and see what needs to be done to get you back on the road. Until then, I will do my best to make you comfortable."

Roxanne was skeptical her version of comfort and Mark's were similar, but she kept her thoughts to herself as he led her from the kitchen to a bathroom the size of a large closet attached to the single bedroom in the back of the cabin.

"It's not much but should have everything you need to get cleaned up. Holler if you need anything." He gave her a small nod and left, closing the door behind him.

Well, this will be interesting. Roxanne took in the bathroom. All the critical items were accounted for—shampoo, conditioner, soap, toothpaste, shower gel, and so on—but none of the product names she saw on the shelves in the shower or over the sink were recognizable. With unfamiliar names and outdoorsy logos, these were products more suitable for the hygiene aisle of a natural food store than the kind of salons Roxanne favored in the city. But for now, she needed to be clean, and so they would have to do.

Luckily, the shower was large and spacious, and the water ran hot. Roxanne dropped her dirty clothes into a heap on the tile floor and stepped in, relishing the way the steam awoke her senses and cleared the mist still clinging to her thoughts. As the fog from her mind lifted, she wondered if she should be more uncomfortable in her present situation—stranded in the snow, with no car, and stuck in an out-of-the-way cabin with a man she hardly knew.

But I don't feel like a stranger here. Everything felt strangely familiar—the snow, the cabin, even Mark himself. Roxanne felt more at home in the little cabin filled with rustic furniture and health-store-brand toiletries than she often did in her swanky apartment in the City.

Okay, you're officially concussed, Roxanne Hudson. Pushing the thought away, she disrobed and stepped into the shower. She scrubbed her body, then switched from soap to face cleanser and washed the remaining bits of her makeup away. She might have smelled like a pinecone, but at least she felt fresh.

Once her shower was finished, Roxanne wrapped her hair with one towel and her body in another. After peeking around the door to make sure the bedroom was unoccupied, she stepped out to see what spare clothes Mark might have assembled for her.

Please don't be flannel. Anything but flannel. Or cable knit.

Nothing made a girl look thick in the shoulders like cable knit.

Roxanne had been so focused on freshening up that she hadn't noticed the bedroom she'd walked through on her way to the tiny bathroom. Like the den and the kitchen before it, the single bedroom—Mark's room, she realized—was modest but nicely appointed. The furniture was large and comfortable-looking, and the bed was covered in a handsome quilt. It looked homemade.

Otherwise, like the rooms she'd seen so far, the bedroom was clean except for random piles of books and a few stray pieces of outdoor equipment. A jacket tossed over a chair in the corner of the room. Her purse laid atop the black and red patchwork quilt, her phone attached to a long white cord that roped its way off the bed, around a bedside table piled high with books, and into an outlet. She was surprised. Not only had Mark been so considerate, he'd had the proper cable for her phone. Hers, of course, had been left in her car.

She plucked her phone from the bed and powered it on. It searched for signal for a few moments before officially declaring none to be found.

Roxanne sighed. She thumbed open her messaging app and tapped out a text to Spencer, hoping it would send automatically whenever the storm passed, and the cell towers came back to life.

You're not going to believe my day. Anything but quaint. Text ya later.

She waited for the message to hit the sending queue, then tossed the phone back onto the bed to complete charging. Beside her purse laid a pair of slim black fleece pants alongside a navy-blue long-sleeved thermal shirt. Neither was terribly fashionable, and both were much too large for her, but they were warm and soft and smelled like Mark. Roxanne didn't waste her time settling into them. She towel-dried her hair, then fished a hair tie from her bag and twisted her damp hair into a messy bun.

It looks like we're going with the boyfriend look. Not exactly her signature style, but it would work. Luckily, she could pull off looking cute in oversized men's clothes with her hair pulled up. All women could, even if they didn't think so.

Meanwhile, Mark had not overlooked any detail. Not only

had he provided her with fresh, clean clothes, but he'd also set out a spare toothbrush and a thick pair of woolen socks with one of those mini candy canes tucked into the cuff as a finishing touch.

This sweet little detail stirred the butterflies in Roxanne's belly, but the boots waiting next to them stopped the lovesick insects mid-flap. Black with quilted nylon, rawhide laces, and a waterproof rubber duck toe, the boots were clean and looked brand new, but suspiciously small, even for Roxanne's size seven and a half. Whoever these boots belonged to, it was definitely not Mark. If he had women's boots lying around at his place, it must mean there was a woman they belonged to somewhere, too. Right?

Roxanne slid the socks over her feet, tugged one side of the thermal shirt over her bare shoulder, and left the boots untouched. She checked her reflection in the dresser mirror, then applied a fresh coat of mascara, and a quick slip of lip gloss from the touch-up kit in her purse. She looked halfway decent, and maybe even more than halfway cute. The look wasn't one she'd wear out, but for a night snowed in with a handsome forest ranger, it would do just fine.

Now, all she had to do was face Mark on the other side of the bedroom door and try to remember he had a pair of ladies' winter boots in his closet, while still trying to sort out funeral arrangements for her relationship somewhere on the other side of the Atlantic.

Besides, she was only snowed in for one night.

Chapter Eight

Roxanne found Mark in the den, tending to the fire. She watched from the doorway as he added a few large logs and extra kindling to the dulling flames. The sounds of crackling wood came from the fireplace, along with flickering light which danced in shadows across Mark's handsome face. He must have brought in the wood from outside, because he was wearing a down jacket open over his charcoal gray shirt and flecks of frost still glistened in his beard. He'd left his snow-caked boots at the door. He was barefoot, and the edges of his jeans were darkened by melted wet. Bogie was still fast asleep on the rug by the hearth, completely undisturbed by his master's work at the fire.

Mark's attention stayed fixed on the fire when she entered, her arrival muffled by the padding of the woolen socks. Roxanne cleared her throat in greeting. He looked up and an expression like surprise passed across his face before he blinked it away and returned to his work. Roxanne shifted in her socks. Had she vastly overestimated the appeal of being dressed in men's clothes?

"Is something wrong?"

"Not at all." He made a noise like a laugh was hiding in his breath. "You just look, well, different."

"It's bad, isn't it?" Roxanne was flustered. Okay, so what she'd thought was the all-natural, fresh-from-the-shower look was apparently playing less boyfriend chic and more homeless girl in oversized clothes and wet hair. She tugged on the shirt and fingered a piece of hair that had fallen loose from her bun. This was more embarrassing than finding herself bundled in a rescue blanket in the snow. What she wouldn't give for a proper tube of lipstick right about now, or one of her own sweaters that knew how to hug her curves. Frumpy was a far cry from fabulous.

Mark leaned the poker against the edge of the stone fireplace. He didn't look at her as he lifted a bellows and breathed air into the fire. "You look …" His voice trailed off as he puffed a few more blows out of the bellows. He seemed to be stuck trying to find the right word.

"That bad?" She fake-laughed to hide her discomfort. If he said yes, it might be worth spending the night freezing in her car rather than warm and humiliated in the cabin.

He squeezed one last breath out of the bellows and let the instrument drop limp between his knees. "Beautiful, actually," he said into the flames. He let the words hang in the air for a moment and busied himself messing with the already brightly burning fire. "You look warm and comfortable," he went on, and swallowed heavily. "I think you're even prettier now than you were before."

"I was pretty before?" Roxanne couldn't stop herself from asking. Mark laughed and she could make out dimples in his profile.

"Very, for someone who was partially frozen."

It took a few moments for the smile to fade enough that she

could force her mouth to move again, and she was grateful Mark kept his attention on the fire. "Thanks for everything you set out for me." Her voice cracked and she swallowed, recovered. "I really appreciate it."

"You're welcome." Mark's tone was huskier than usual. He dusted off his knees as he rose beside her.

He smiled down at her, and there was something different about the way he looked at her. Roxanne couldn't quite describe it, but she could *feel* it, earnest and pulsing as it lingered in the lower parts of her stomach. She felt warm suddenly—warmer than she should have been, even with the winter clothes and roaring fire—and Mark's eyes were such a dazzling shade of green as they stared into hers. She was sure she'd never seen such a hue before, which was saying something for a woman who stared at color swatches for hours every day.

"Everything fits okay?" His lips were so close and his words so deep they nearly vibrated against hers when he spoke. The pair seemed to be falling toward each other, though neither of them was trying.

What came out Roxanne's mouth was supposed to be yes, but it was lost on a rush of breath. She tried again. "Everything is great." Desperate to find a way out of his heat before she melted, she ducked her head. "You thought of everything. I had no idea your feet were so small, though. You might wear a shoe size smaller than me."

She hadn't meant to throw in the last part about the boots, but apparently her subconscious had other plans.

Great job, Roxanne. Way to wreck the mood.

Mark's eyebrows crinkled as he drew back, and then a smile

softened them back into place. "Maggie's."

He pointed to the mantel behind Roxanne's head and plucked up a silver picture frame, then turned it around so she could see the photo of Mark with his arms wrapped around the shoulders of a lovely brunette. He tapped his finger against the glass, against the image of the woman. "My sister, Maggie."

Roxanne studied the photograph. Maggie had the same dark hair as Mark, the same green eyes, the same easy smile. Maggie's face was slimmer, and she had a dimple in her cheek, but the familial resemblance was undeniable.

"Twins?"

"Yep." Mark shrugged out of his jacket and tossed it away onto the armchair with his free hand. He smiled down at the picture. "She comes out this way sometimes around the holidays. Never met a girl who loves the snow as much as Mags does—this blizzard would be like her own personal Heaven."

For the first time, Roxanne remembered she wasn't the only one going home for the holidays. Her hand fluttered to her chin. "Oh. Is she coming for Christmas? What about the rest of your family?" The worrisome feeling she'd imposed on him at the worst possible time flooded her, extinguishing the heat that had been building between them. "I haven't ruined your holiday plans, have I? I'm so sorry."

His eyebrows up, Mark caught her hand where it hovered and held it. "Not at all. Mags is off sailing around the world. She's probably somewhere in the southern seas by now."

Roxanne eyed him suspiciously, and he squeezed her hand again.

"She's a professor for Semester at Sea, so coming home for the holidays isn't always on the itinerary. You haven't inconvenienced me at all, Roxy." He stared into her eyes for a moment too long, and then released her hand, moving backward and returning the frame to its home on the mantel.

Roxanne's eyes narrowed, and Mark noticed. "Did I say something wrong?"

"Nobody calls me Roxy but my dad."

"Oh." He chewed at his lip and raised an eyebrow in supplication. "I apologize if I overstepped."

"It's not that." Normally, Roxanne despised the nickname, but she didn't mind the sound of it sliding off the handsome ranger's lips. "I kind of like it." She cleared her throat and routed the conversation back to a safer subject. "So, what about your parents? Are they coming for the holidays?"

Mark directed his answer at the photograph of him and his sister. "They passed away a long time ago," he said. "Just me and Mags now. Or just me and Bogie, I guess."

"I'm so sorry," Roxanne said automatically, and meant it. Her chest grew heavy as thoughts of her own family crept into her mind. How much time did one take for granted when they thought they had the luxury of forever? She'd taken three years—three years of excuses not to visit for the holidays, of few phone calls and even fewer visits, all under the guide of focusing on her career. Even when her dad had called to ask her to come home for the holidays, told her this might me Grandma Myrtle's last Christmas, she'd never actually stopped to think about how she'd feel if they weren't there. If this truly was the *last* year they could all be together.

Had it been worth it? How much had she missed—and for what, a few scrapped designs and a relationship she couldn't hold together with all the stitching in the world?

Mark gave her an easy smile that was soft enough to ease the tension in her chest. "It was a long time ago but thank you."

"So—" She rocked on her feet, having a hard time making eye contact again. "What's next?"

He smiled. "Well, if you're up for it, maybe you could help Santa get ready for Christmas." He gestured over at the undecorated fir tree and the half-opened boxes of assorted decorations.

Behind these, Roxanne inspected the boxes of parcels she'd noticed before. Various children's toys and books, and several pieces of children's clothing waited for wrapping. Her eyes widened as Mark walked over and began pulling more bags of unwrapped gifts out from behind the tree. He hadn't been kidding about Santa—there were easily enough gifts to fill a sleigh. How had she not noticed them before?

"What is all that?" Roxanne asked as several rolls of festive wrapping paper and ribbon spilled out from behind the tree, thumping on the wooden floor alongside a landslide of tissue paper that slid free of its tower. "Are you running deliveries in your snow-cat-mobile or something?"

"It's called a snowcat," he corrected her, shaking his head. "And something like that. These toys are for the Green Mountain Patrol's ranger toy drive. Lots of poor folks on the edge of these mountains. Most couldn't get out for the holidays even if they could afford it. So, around September, we start collecting, and every year on Christmas Eve—or the day before if the weather's tricky—I get everything wrapped up, put on the big red suit, and ride out on the *snowcat*." He exaggerated the word, winking as he did. "And do my best to play Santa. Somebody's got to deliver out to all the kids in Vermont, too."

Roxanne was touched, and if she hadn't already been looking at the ranger with adoration, she certainly was now. She thought about his last words—that Santa had to deliver in Vermont—and chuckled, remembering what Spencer had said back in the office.

"What's so funny? Don't think I can pull off Santa with this measly excuse for a beard, do you?" Mark teased, stroking the thin strip of beard on his jaw. Then, lifting a plush reindeer with a bright red plastic nose from one of the boxes, he addressed it in mock jest. "Roxy doesn't think I can pull off Santa, Rudolph."

Elsewhere in the room, Bogie huffed in his sleep, adding to the conversation.

"No, it's not that!" Roxanne laughed, enjoying the silly moment. "You reminded me of something my friend Spencer said before I left New York is all."

Something like disappointment flashed across Mark's face, gone as quickly as she'd seen it. "Boyfriend?"

Roxanne got the impression he was trying to sound disinterested.

"No, definitely not. Wrong team," she explained. "He'd been teasing me—" Roxanne stopped mid-sentence. Spencer had been teasing her about Santa bringing her a new mountain man for Christmas, and this was not something she was exactly eager to share when snowed in with, and wearing the borrowed clothes of, Vermont's most handsome and philanthropic ranger.

"Teasing you about what?" Mark coaxed. He turned Rudolph so the stuffed animal echoed the question. "This Spencer doesn't think the big guy in red delivers out here in the boonies?"

"Oh, it was nothing." Roxanne waved Mark's words—and Rudolph's stare—away. "Nonsense about spending the holidays up in Vermont. But it looks like I'm all yours for the night, so put me to work, Santa."

Mark eyed the clock, then stooped to pick up a roll of wrapping paper—red and white candy cane stripe. "It's late. You sure you're up for it?"

Roxanne grinned, the memory of her late-night holiday baking sprees still fresh in her mind, and reached for the paper. "I'm not sure I could fall asleep right now, not after all the excitement of the evening. Besides, isn't it bad to go to bed with a concussion?"

"Monitoring throughout the night is prudent after a head injury," he agreed, before a wide smile spread across his face. "Besides, I've got just the thing to keep us awake."

Chapter Nine

"This is one of the most delicious things I've ever eaten in my life," Roxanne said, scooping another forkful of sweet maple pie into her mouth. Creamy and decadent, the taste swelled on her tongue, inviting bite after bite. "I can't believe I've never had this before."

"Maple syrup pie is a Vermont delicacy," Mark agreed. "Have to admit I didn't make this one myself, though."

"No?" Roxanne helped herself to another bite. Normally she wouldn't think of doing a thing, but the sugar had made her reckless. At least she was wearing pants with an elastic waistband. What were the holidays without a little bit of junk food, anyway? New Year's resolutions would be so much less predictable if people didn't eat themselves silly for the holidays.

"It was a gift from a coworker's mother. She bakes pies for all the rangers at the holidays," Mark explained as he served himself another slice.

"Then my compliments to the chef."

When they'd polished off the pie, Mark poured them both mugs of bourbon-spiked hot cocoa and strung a set of frosted white lights on the tree for ambiance, while Roxanne was tasked with selecting music.

She held up two 45s. "What do you prefer? *Crooners Christmas* or *A Very Piano Yuletide?*"

"Guest's choice."

Roxanne placed the instrumental album on the turntable and set it at a low volume. The popping sounds of the record player added another layer of music to the crackling of the fire as they set about the task of wrapping the toy-drive presents. It took them hours, not that they minded the time, and they worked steadily, sometimes talking, sometimes lapsing into a comfortable silence as they concentrated on attaching ribbons and bows to the children's gifts.

All the while, snow continued to fall, blanketing the earth in an ever-deepening coat of white. Once or twice they'd open the door to peek out, and every time Roxanne felt a little more positive toward the falling snow, which showed no sign of letting up. Each time they opened the door, Mark stood a little closer to her, and along with his body heat Roxanne could swear she heard sleigh bells ringing in the distance. For the first time in as long as she could remember—and perhaps it was just a consequence of the bourbon and cocoa—she could feel herself being truly caught up in the holiday spirit.

"Do you hear that?" It was their third trip on the porch, and Roxanne still heard the tinkling of jingle bells with every flurry of falling snow.

"Hear what?" Mark slid closer, blocking the wind. The later it got, the gustier the wind had become, until it had grown so strong and loud it almost had a voice of its own.

Roxanne didn't mind. It made Mark lean in closer and whisper in her ear as a result, and she was enjoying the closeness. "I keep hearing something," she said.

Mark's face twisted with worry. He stooped to stare into her eyes. "Are you still hearing that ringing noise?" Concern sharpened his tone as he examined her pupils.

"No, not like that." She fumbled for a better way to explain what she was hearing. "This sounds like bells. Sleigh bells, to be specific."

"Santa doesn't come for another night or two, you know," Mark teased, relaxing. "Are you so eager for Christmas?"

She elbowed him in the ribs playfully, ignoring the suspicious way he looked at her. "No," she laughed. "I'm not really a … Christmas person. Maybe I hit my head harder than I thought."

"Not a Christmas person? What does that mean, exactly?" Mark touched a finger to the side of his nose and furrowed his brow as if in deep thought. "Is it all the presents you don't enjoy? Or perhaps the warm feeling of the company of family and friends? The lights? Snowmen?"

"No—"

Roxanne tried to protest, but Mark waved her away as he continued to name all the wonderful things about the season.

"Must be the cookies or the cocoa," he continued, ignoring the jab of her elbow when she nudged him a second time. He snapped his fingers. "I've got it. It's Santa, isn't it—the big guy himself? You don't buy into the whole magic of Christmas thing? Worried Roxanne Hudson didn't make her way onto the nice list this year?"

He was impossible, and Roxanne felt a bit guilty about the bad rap she'd been giving the holiday. Still, she couldn't give up her position now.

"Not even a little," she fibbed. Maybe it was the sudden fun she was having, or maybe it was the concussion, but there was something different about the holidays this year. How quickly things had changed—from dreading the trip to Vermont, to being rescued in a blizzard by a ranger, this Christmas was turning out to be the polar opposite of anything Roxanne had expected.

With a little help from the bourbon, they talked, laughed, and enjoyed several heart-palpating moments when their hands would brush while reaching for another present to wrap. When neither of them could hold their eyes open any longer, and the sky had begun to pale into pre-dawn, they finally agreed it was time to call it a night.

"I'll be right back."

Mark excused himself to the bathroom, leaving Roxanne to sit nervously on the couch, fidgeting with the edge of a knit blanket and fretting over sleeping arrangements. She had gotten so caught up in the magic of the evening it had been easy to forget she was a guest here. This wasn't home.

A warm muzzle set itself on Roxanne's thigh. "I guess it's time for bed, Bogie."

Bogie wagged his tail and yawned, then began to shuffle slowly toward the bedroom. At the threshold, he bumped open the door with his nose and wedged his way through. In the open space,

Roxanne could see Mark moving about, a pillow in one hand and a bright blue toothbrush clenched between his teeth. Roxanne barely noticed either of the items. She was too busy trying to pick her jaw up off the floor.

Mark had traded his jeans in for plaid flannel pajama bottoms and lost his shirt. He was currently trying to wrangle a plain white tee over his head with one hand. *It's not polite to stare*, Roxanne scolded herself, but she did anyway, watching, mesmerized as the taut, well-defined muscles of Mark's stomach rippled beneath the swell of pecs that looked like they'd be a far more comfortable resting place than any pillow she'd ever slept on. How did he have so many abs? He had at least eight fully defined muscles in his abdomen, and they all moved in one well-choreographed mass as his stomach dipped and sliced downward, disappearing beneath the precariously low waistband of his pants. His shoulders were broad, and there wasn't an inch of fat on his chiseled body. His skin was, as was the rest of him, tanned and flawless.

Roxanne gulped. Her cheeks were on fire. *Oh my.* She was no stranger to gorgeous men. She saw beautiful people every day roaming the hallways of *Divine* headquarters. Yet, something about Mark made Roxanne's breath catch in her throat.

She made a mental note to give Bogie an extra scratch behind the ear for bumping open the door and diverted her gaze as Mark slipped the shirt over his head. By the time he pushed his way through the bedroom door and back into the living room, he'd tugged the shirt down over his chest and torso, eclipsing Roxanne's view.

"Everything all right?" If Mark suspected she'd gotten a glimpse, it didn't show. Finished brushing his teeth, he waved his toothbrush at her to get her attention.

"Just peachy." Roxanne winced at the silly statement.

Mark dropped his pillow on the couch between them, and sat at the opposite end, reclining with his feet propped up on the coffee table. He rolled his head to the side and smiled at Roxanne, and she pulled her knees against her chest as their gazes wandered to the Christmas tree. What had started off as a bare pine with boxes of decorations and presents underneath had erupted into packages of brightly colored wrapping paper, glittery bows, and twinkling lights. Mark had hung a mismatched pair of stockings—one with his name embroidered on the cuff, the other with his sister's—on the mantel alongside Bogie's.

"You know," he ventured, rolling his eyes to Roxanne, "for someone who's not the biggest fan of Christmas, you sure do wrap a mean present."

She laughed. "Reason 7,941 I dislike the holidays: four straight seasons of working the gift wrap station at Macy's."

"Ah. A veteran wrapper."

Roxanne nodded. "Good tips. Helped me pay my way through college."

"Not still whiling away your days at Macy's, I take it?"

"No." In all their conversations over the course of the evening, Roxanne had managed to almost completely avoid talking about herself. "I'm a senior fashion editor at *Divine*. I started at the copy desk, and now I have my own column." She felt a surge of pride. "I was in Milan this year for Milan Fashion Week. I wore Valentino."

Mark blinked, but there was no hint of recognition in them. He smiled anyway. "It sounds like you love your job."

Roxanne nodded enthusiastically—maybe a little too enthusiastically. "I do. I've still got a long way to go, but I'm happy with how far I've come. Everyone says I'm on track to climb up, but what I'm really hoping to do is to get into design myself." She realized she was talking too much and stopped. "What about you? Did you always know you wanted to be a park ranger?"

Mark shrugged. "More or less. When you spend enough time hopping around, city after city, you come to enjoy the peace and quiet."

"Did you move a lot before?"

"After our parents died, Mags and I were in and out of foster care for a while."

Roxanne had at least a dozen questions queuing up, but she didn't dare ask any of them.

"New York, Boston, Chicago ... Kind of bounced around, going anywhere as long as we could stay together," Mark explained. "When it finally came time for me to decide where I wanted to go, all I wanted was to get as far away from everything as possible. Mags too, but she was the type to keep moving, not find somewhere and settle in. She's done everything from Peace Corps to Semester at Sea. I took a job as a seasonal ranger out of college and spent some time in Denali and Yellowstone before falling in love with the Green Mountains. Haven't left Vermont since. Summers here are beautiful; so is fall. Winter is my favorite, though. Everything is white, and so still you can almost feel nature holding its breath for spring."

Roxanne wasn't sure what to say, so she added more of herself to the conversation. "I grew up in a small suburb in Connecticut. Went to Pratt, and then moved to Manhattan and bounced around a little until I got hired at *Divine*. You haven't seen summer until you've spent it in the City—the concerts and summer festivals in Central Park are amazing. I have one sister, Rachel. She's still in Connecticut, married with a small flock of children."

Mark chuckled. "Sound like polar opposites, like me and Mags."

"Who, you and me? Or me and Rachel?"

"Well, both I guess … although, I don't think you and I are too different. Not really."

It was Roxanne's turn to chuckle. "You don't? Vermont versus New York City, winter versus summer. Come on."

Mark's mouth stretched into a fake grimace, and he clicked his tongue against his teeth. "I don't know, Roxy. I think you might like it here in the woods a little more than you're letting on."

"Oh, is that right?"

He rose from the couch, reaching for her with both hands. She accepted them, and he lifted her to her feet. With a squeeze, Mark released Roxanne's fingers and tapped one of his fingertips to his head. "I've got a sense about these things."

The way he smiled at her made Roxanne's insides melt.

"I'm off to bed. I'll take the couch and you take my bed. The sun will be up soon, and we'll head out first thing to your car, bring your things back. While you get ready, I'll load up my sleigh for the toy delivery, then drop you off at your family's cabin on my way out."

"Thank you," Roxanne said, grateful for everything Mark had done for her. "But I don't want to kick you out of your bed. I'm fine with the couch."

"Not a chance. I would completely lose my gentleman card if

I left a lady to sleep on this lumpy old thing. Besides"—he jerked his head in Bogie's direction, asleep on the floor—"it smells like dog," he said, laying his hands atop her shoulders to steer her toward the bedroom. "Good night, Roxanne."

She smiled, thinking of the lush pillow and thick quilt that awaited her. She was exhausted. "Good night, Mark."

Just as she crossed the threshold into the bedroom, Mark called her back. "Hey, Roxy?"

"Yes?"

"I wouldn't totally dismiss the idea of Christmas magic, not yet," he said, settling himself onto the couch, adjusting cushions and pillows and dragging a blanket over his chest. "You never know—Santa might have something planned for you."

Chapter Ten

oxanne slept soundly and woke up thinking of the forest and craving sugar plums. She used a musky vanilla fabric spray on her sheets at home, but Mark's bed was rich with his woodsy scent, and it felt homier than hers did, which was as surprising as it was refreshing. Fresh morning light filtered in through curtains on the bedroom window, and the air was scented with fresh coffee and cinnamon.

Rubbing the sleep from her eyes, Roxanne pulled herself out of bed and stumbled to the small bathroom without bothering to look at her phone. It was early, she could tell without checking the time, and it was the day before Christmas Eve. Nobody emailed two days before the biggest holiday of the year, right? The holiday was officially here.

She brushed her teeth to get rid of the dragon breath and gave her face a quick wash with cool water from the faucet, then brushed out her hair and tamed the wild fly-aways from last night's wet bun into a more reasonable low ponytail.

Mark was in the kitchen. His hair stuck up in wayward tufts, and he was wearing his jacket unzipped over a plain long-sleeved shirt and a pair of bright blue snow pants. He was pulling a tray out of the oven as Roxanne arrived in the kitchen. When he looked up at her, the sunlight pouring in through the kitchen window made his eyes even more brilliantly green.

"Morning," she greeted. "Something smells delicious."

"Well, good morning." He smiled as he set a plate of cinnamon rolls on the table and plucked an empty coffee mug from the rack hanging above the counter. He poured her a cup of coffee and set it next to the plate of steaming pastries, then motioned toward bowls of cream and sugar. "Don't get too excited," he said when she bypassed the coffee and reached for a cinnamon roll. "Coffee is fresh ground, but the cinnamon rolls are from a can. Figured you might like something more substantial for breakfast than a bit of granola and a strip of cowboy jerky."

"Are you kidding?" she teased. "I didn't know there were other things to have for breakfast besides coffee."

Mark chuckled and poured himself a cup of fresh coffee, then dumped in a heavy glug of milk until the black liquid turned cream. "Sometimes you have to treat yourself."

After doing a quick mental calculation of the caloric intake of a cinnamon roll, Roxanne reached for the smallest of the bunch. Loosening the dietary shackles a tiny bit didn't mean she could let go of herself completely. She took a bite of the pastry, savoring the sticky sweetness as it melted on her tongue, and swallowed. "It's amazing. I woke up with a sweet craving. Totally on carb overload after the pie last night, though."

"Doesn't count," Mark said, picking up a roll for himself and cupping one hand underneath it as he took a bite. "That was yesterday. You'll work it off today in the snow anyway."

"Oh, right!" She had almost forgotten that getting her things from her car would require a trip back through the snow, and this time Mark wouldn't be carrying her. "Is it a long walk back to my car? How far is it?"

"Not far at all," he grinned, pointing toward the living room.

Roxanne looked in the direction he was pointing and saw her suitcase waiting at the back door.

"I hope you don't mind, but I still had your car keys in my pocket, and you were sleeping, so I trekked out there this morning with the old man and took care of everything. Figured you didn't have the gear for the hike anyway. Your bags are in the living room defrosting. Anything else you need, I'm sure Maggie has a pair left around here somewhere you can borrow."

Roxanne's jaw dropped. "Oh my gosh, you're kidding! You didn't have to do that. I would have gone with you—you should have woken me up."

He shrugged and took a sip of coffee. "You *did* have an accident yesterday, you know. You needed the sleep, and Bogie and I enjoy a good morning hike anyway. He needs the exercise. Plus, I'm an early riser. My pleasure, I promise."

While she was grateful, again, for Mark's consideration, and relieved she could soon get back into her own clothes, Roxanne almost regretted missing the walk in the snow with her favorite stranger. Sure, she hated hiking, and a trek through the deluge of snow that had accumulated overnight sounded like a special sort of torture, but it was hard to imagine *not* enjoying taking the walk with Mark. Then she remembered it hadn't only been the suitcase they'd been after.

"How bad is the damage to my car?" She tried not to wince

when she asked, but the BMW *was* virtually brand new, and repairs would undoubtedly be expensive.

"Surprisingly minimal. In fact, almost nonexistent. Some ice in the grill, but I got it out. Maybe a ding here or there in the hood, but you'd have to look to find it. The softness of the snow really did you a favor. Needs a little digging out, but everything appears shipshape."

"That's amazing news. I'm so glad I won't have to deal with major repairs." Roxanne stuffed the last of the cinnamon roll in her mouth and poured herself a cup of coffee, breathing in the rich scent. It smelled like hazelnut and would pair wonderfully with the pastry. "I still wish I knew what ran out in front of me."

"Could have been a deer. Could have been Santa." Mark winked at her. "Never know this time of year."

Roxanne swallowed her laugh down with another sip of coffee. Whatever it was, she was kind of glad she'd swerved—otherwise she'd have made it to the cabin on time and missed out on Mark, which seemed a tragedy. "So, are we ready to head out?"

Mark rubbed at his eyebrow, a red tinge crawling back out from under his beard. "Unfortunately, the storm was worse than we thought. I don't think we're going to be getting too far out in that, even in the snowcat. Too thick, and too much shine on the snow. Needs a little time to settle."

"What does that mean?" Roxanne asked, mentally doing the math. Another day in the cabin with Mark wasn't anything close to terrible, but tomorrow was Christmas Eve.

"It means we're snowed in for another day. I'm sorry. I know I promised you I'd get you home—"

"Don't be," Roxanne cut in. "I'm just glad you'll let me stay another night."

Mark grinned at her over his coffee mug. "Only if you promise to earn your keep."

"Oh? What does that mean?" The way he was smiling at her made Roxanne's insides flutter—in a good way.

He set down the mug down, but his grin got even wider. "If we're going to be snowed in, we're going to need to keep the fire blazing. Want to help me chop some firewood?"

Roxanne had, of course, never chopped firewood. At first, she'd balked at the thought, worried about what slinging around heavy piece of wood and iron might do to her manicure. The second she felt the ax in her hand, though, all worry faded away.

"You're a natural," Mark said as Roxanne swung the ax again, slicing another thick log in half. She looked at her progress, impressed with her own work. Her arms ached and she was in need of a shower, but she'd managed to transform a pile of logs into a stack of processed firework. Mark had tried to step in half a dozen times but chopping firewood had been the best workout she'd had in weeks—and the best therapy. Three logs down and it'd been hard to remember what she'd been so stressed about when she'd left the City. By the time she'd split six logs, she'd almost decided she wasn't going back. She'd just stay in the woods. Heck, she might even wear flannel.

Roxanne wiped snowflakes and sweat off her brow, then shrugged. "Piece of cake."

"I've seen what you can do to cake."

"Pie," she corrected, recalling the sweet taste of maple cream. "You've seen what I can do to *pie.*"

"Same thing."

"It is not the same thing," Roxanne insisted, brandishing the ax.

He laughed and tossed up his hands. "Okay, you're right—it's not the same thing." He bent to collect the pieces of newly sliced log, adding them to the pile of firewood. "One has crust."

Roxanne positioned another log on the cutting stump and lifted the ax. A stitch pulled in her back, and she reached behind to rub it loose.

"Hey, hold on a second."

She glanced at the log as Mark moved behind her. "Am I doing something wrong?"

"Not at all, but let me help you fix your posture so you don't throw your back out. I didn't specify I'd deliver you home uninjured, but it was sort of implied."

One of Roxanne's hands moved reflexively to her lower back. "Have I been doing it wrong this entire time?"

Laughing, Mark wrapped himself around Roxanne, then used his hands to pivot her hips so one foot was a little ahead of the other and her back was straight.

"Not at all, but if you're going to keep swinging, we need to level you up." He put his hands atop hers, adjusting her right hand toward the head of the ax and her left lower at the knob. "Got it?" he asked as he guided her arms to mimic the motion of the swing. "As the ax comes down, slide your right hand down and move into the swing. Let the momentum flow through you, instead of pull you into it."

With his body pressed against hers, Roxanne barely heard what he said. It took her a few times to make her lips shape words and she didn't manage to force them out until Mark had moved away, leaving nothing but cold behind her. "Got it."

She swung again and the blade fell smoothly downward. The log split in half, and nothing pinched in her back. Inspired, she reached for another log and Mark laughed.

"That was the last log."

"You're kidding."

"Nope. We've got enough firewood to last the rest of the winter now. You should have crashed your car in the snow in my neck of the woods sooner."

Roxanne rolled her eyes playfully and let the ax head drop in the snow. "Now what?"

"Lunch."

"It's already lunch time?" Roxanne's stomach growled, which was unusual. She was lucky to get a pre-packaged salad from the lunch trolley when she was at work, and even then, it was risky. Nobody wanted to risk mid-afternoon bloat in her line of business.

Mark tossed away the remainder of the firewood, then tucked several pieces under his arm and motioned in the direction of the house. "As crazy as it seems, it's already mid-afternoon," he confirmed. "Nothing works up an appetite like chopping firewood."

Roxanne's stomach growled again. She was famished—a level of hunger she'd never once assigned herself.

While she cleaned up, Mark tended to the fire. By the time she'd settled on an outfit appropriate for lounging around indoors but still fashionable enough to impress, Mark had already prepared two sandwiches and set the table.

More carbs, she thought, but said, "That looks amazing," and settled into her chair. Thank goodness she'd burned off some Christmas calories while out chopping firewood. She bit back a laugh. Would Spencer still call her quaint if he saw her wielding an ax?

"But how does it taste?"

Roxanne took a bite and chewed, the delicious flavors playing on her tongue. "Wow."

"I call it a B.A.T. sandwich."

Midway through a second bite, Roxanne froze. She contemplated the flavors. "Bacon, avocado, and tomato."

Mark raised his sandwich in salute. "I never liked lettuce."

"Me either," she admitted, all those stolen lunchtime salads forgotten. "You're a culinary genius."

"You're easy to please."

Roxanne considered as she chewed. Had anyone else said that, she might have been offended, or at least assumed it was a backhanded compliment. From Mark, it sounded genuine.

"Do you think so? I mean, you don't think I'm high maintenance?"

He swallowed down a bite and shook his head. "Not at all. Why?"

"No reason." She remembered how judgmental she'd been about his off-brand hygiene products.

"You know, guys can be high maintenance, too."

A vision of Hunter wafted into her head, followed on its heels by Spencer in his meticulously pressed shirt and perfectly cut hair.

"Don't I know it."

She swallowed her last bite of sandwich, but found she was still hungry. "Let me cook dinner for you?" she asked. The question popped out of her mouth before she could think better of it. She knew how to order take out. She did *not* know how to cook.

Mark started to protest. "You're a guest—"

"Please. To say thank you."

"I was defrosting a couple of steaks …"

"Perfect." How hard could it be to cook a steak?

Chapter Eleven

Cooking a steak dinner was, in fact, a lot harder than Roxanne had expected. She'd managed to fill up the kitchen with smoke when Mark burst in from gathering more firewood outside, Bogie ambling hot on his heels.

"Roxanne!" he called.

"It's okay, I got it," Roxanne lied as she tried desperately to wave away smoke with a dishrag. She didn't have it. More smoke wafted out of the oven. How embarrassing.

Mark reached over her head to turn on the exhaust fan, then pushed open the window over the sink and used his arms to expel smoke. "Are you all right?"

"I'm fine." Roxanne grimaced as she pulled a pan of burnt potatoes from the oven and set them on top of the stove beside her tray of hockey puck steaks. "But dinner isn't."

"I was in the mood for a salad anyway."

She spun on him, her eyes narrowed. "You said you don't like lettuce."

He bit back a smile. "Not on sandwiches. Put it in a bowl with tomatoes and cucumbers …" His voice trailed off as Roxanne continued to glower. "And broccoli and carrots …"

Roxanne realized he was teasing and managed a smile. "I'm sorry. I'm a terrible cook, apparently."

"But an excellent lumberjack," he reassured her. "Honestly, Roxy, you can serve me a bowl of rocks and I'll be happy—as long as I'm sitting across from you."

She grinned. "The steaks are hard as rocks."

"You've already sold me on a salad. No takebacks."

Steaks and potatoes consigned to the garbage, they made a simple supper of salad and another serving of maple pie, and afterward retired back to the couch in the den. The space had been cozy the night before, but after a day of hard work and decorating, it was a home fit for the holidays. The tree had been trimmed, the fire lit, and as Roxanne settled into the overstuffed cushions, Mark emerged from the kitchen carrying two mugs of hot chocolate, both topped with a swirl of whipped cream.

"You keep this up and I'm not going to want to leave," she said, accepting one of the mugs.

Mark winked as he settled onto the other end of the couch. "Maybe that's the plan. In the mood for a holiday movie?"

"What did you have in mind?"

He patted the cushion and stroked Bogie's ears as they appeared at the edge of the couch.

"Oh, I was thinking something classic—something quintessentially Christmas."

Roxanne groaned into her cocoa and Mark directed his next question at the dog. "What do you think, old man?"

Bogie wagged his tail and emitted a low *woof.*

"Ah, yes," Mark said, as if her understood the dog's language perfectly. "Good choice."

Roxanne giggled, enjoying the interaction between the two as Mark rose and moved to the shelf of DVDs, running his finger along the titles.

"Either one of you boys want to tell me what we're watching?"

Bogie responded by settling his snout on her leg. He rolled his big brown eyes up at her, and she scratched at his ear. Why had she never gotten a dog?

Because Hunter's allergic. She'd nearly forgotten.

"A true seasonal classic," Mark narrated as he selected the film and set the shiny disc into the movie player, then clicked on the television. Old time music played and a dark-haired man wearing a tattered jacket appeared on screen, followed by the film's title: *We're No Angels.*

"Bogart," Roxanne laughed. Bogie nudged her thigh, soliciting another rub. She cocked her thumb at the dog and dropped her voice in her best Bogart impression. "Here's lookin' at you, kid."

"And you said you didn't like Christmas," Mark jested.

"*We're No Angels* is hardly a Christmas film." Roxanne tsked. She fidgeted on the cushion, first tucking one leg under and then the other. She decided on the first and shifted to lean again the arm rest.

"What are you talking about? It's absolutely a Christmas film."

"Just because it takes place over the holidays doesn't make it a Christmas film," she argued, then adjusted her legs again. "I'm sorry, this cushion is a little bumpy," she explained when she caught Mark peering at her from the corner of his eye.

"Do you want to switch?"

"Oh, no." Roxanne pressed the empty cushion between them, and shot a mischievous look at Mark. "This one is more comfortable, I think."

Mark watched as she arranged herself on the middle seat, snuggling in close at his side. When she had quieted, she felt his arm drape over her shoulders just as Humphrey Bogart and his two rowdy companions sauntered up the streets of a French colonial town, looking for trouble. Bogie's snout found its way back into her lap, and Roxanne breathed in Mark's warm pine scent, her gaze moving from the television to the soft glow of the tree lights. "Yeah, this is much better."

They breakfasted the next morning on leftover pie. Afterward, Roxanne showered and did her hair and makeup, dressing in the warmest outfit she had packed for her trip—black leather leggings and an oversized eggshell cashmere sweater with a few layers of chenille scarves. She considered her shiny patent leather ankle boots but opted for Mag's borrowed wet-weather boots instead and pulled her beanie over her hair.

She checked her reflection in the mirror in Mark's bedroom.

"Welcome back," she told her reflection. She was relieved to see Roxanne Hudson, *Divine* Fashion Editor looking back at her, and not the haphazard girl with messy hair and men's clothing. That look had worked yesterday, but today was a new day— Christmas Eve. She had to get to her family's house and show them a career in fashion was a lifestyle, not a hobby. And she wanted to look good for Mark. Everything below her waist looked *amazing* in these pants.

It's almost time to say goodbye. The thought sucked the joy out of her mood. Maybe she could invite Mark to Christmas dinner with her parents. They knew him, and it wasn't like he had other plans. It wouldn't be a date, she reasoned. She owed him for saving her and putting her up, and the dinner she'd cooked—*attempted* to cook—had been a bust. An invite to a holiday feast would be a proper thank you.

"Ready when you are," Mark called from the den, breaking into her thoughts. He'd been in and out of the house, a string of bells on the back door announcing his comings and goings as he loaded the snowcat with the gifts for the children's toy drive. "No hurry. Take your time."

"I'm coming," she called back, tossing her coat over her shoulder before slipping the zipper on her overnight bag closed. She took one last look in the mirror, flipped her hair, and checked her lipstick. Yeah, her legs looked amazing in these leather leggings. A little much for a family holiday, but trés chic.

Mark's eyes bugged out when Roxanne strode through the doorway and into the den, hoisting her heavy bag on her shoulder. In an instant he was in front of her, reaching for the luggage.

"Welcome back, Ms. New York." The slight smile he was wearing didn't match the husky quality in his voice.

Something about it made Roxanne blush. She preened, just a little. "You say it like it's a bad thing."

"Not at all."

His hand brushed her shoulder as he withdrew the bag, and for a moment he lifted his hand like he might touch her face.

Roxanne could feel the heat pulsing from his fingers, rising toward her. She shifted, barely, and rolled her eyes up to meet his as she felt her lips soften into a pucker.

"Cold." Mark's voice cracked, and he pulled back his hand, letting it fall at his side as he took a step backward. He cleared his throat and tried again. "It's cold out. Might be a little too cold for you, unless you're hiding a snowsuit under that sweater. We need to get you bundled up. You'd make a lovely ice sculpture, but I don't think you'd enjoy the experience."

The flirt in her started to protest, but then the realist kicked in. She showed him the coat, fully prepared to list off its designer qualities once more, but the look on his face was the same passive, unconvinced one he'd worn the last time, so she shrugged. "This is all I brought," she sighed. "You don't happen to have a coat of Maggie's I could borrow for the ride, do you?"

Mark made a clicking sound with his tongue. "She has some extra outdoor gear in the linen closet in the kitchen. Coat and some gloves. I'll go grab them."

At the doorway to the kitchen, he stopped and put his palm on the wall, looking at her over his shoulder. "Oh, by the way, the cell towers seem to be back up and all clear. Check your phone. You might have service now if you want to check in with anyone."

Roxanne reached into her Louis Vuitton and pulled out her iPhone, then held the little round button until the screen lit up with life. She waited patiently, listening as Mark rummaged around in closets unseen. When her phone's background—a press photo of Hunter and her at a junket for last season's fall line—appeared on screen, the image looked different from the last time she'd seen it.

Hunter looked dashing as always, his trim European tailored suit as perfectly styled as his wave of sandy blond hair. She had worn a Hepburn-inspired LBD with off-the-shoulder sleeves, a full high-low skirt, and crystals and pearls everywhere she could stick them. They'd both been perfect that night, no doubt about that, but for the first time, Roxanne saw beyond the façade. The smile on Hunter's profile as he looked at her and the way he had his arm slung low around her back weren't evidence of his love for her, but a polished, camera-ready pose. The grin on Roxanne's face was so forced it was almost a wince. How had she ever liked this photo? Everything about it looked so ... uncomfortable.

She waited, but no new text messages came through—not even anything from Spencer. Of course, she hadn't expected to hear from Hunter, but he had known she'd been driving out of state in her brand-new car that had never left the parking garage. He should have checked in on her, right? Her inbox lagged, the signal still too weak to refresh her email. She thought about thumbing open one of her social media apps and seeing if that would update but decided any against it. Tonight was Christmas Eve.

Roxanne was still staring indecisively at the picture on her phone when Mark's concerned voice interrupted her thoughts.

"Is something wrong?"

"No." She slipped her phone back into her bag. "Nothing."

Mark smiled, too polite to press the matter, and walked toward her, holding out a thick coat and other assorted winter accessories. "These certainly aren't as fashionable as you're used to, but they'll keep you warm and comfortable out in the snow."

Roxanne accepted the gear and cast a final look around the

cabin. The room which had been so foreign to her had become rich with warm memories. Sweet maple pie in the kitchen. Warm bourbon by the crackling fire. Laughter as she and Mark had wrapped gift after gift under the tree they'd strung with lights and garland. Bogie's head on her knee. Mark's eyes on her as she watched the snow. The feel of his arm around her on the couch.

She wasn't ready for it all to end. Not yet.

An idea popped in her mind. "Hey, do you think instead of going straight to the cabin, maybe I could tag along and help you deliver presents?"

He arched an eyebrow and gave her a teasing smirk. "And here I thought you might never get into the spirit. I'm so pleased you've decided to renounce your Grinchy ways, Roxanne Hudson. I was a bit worried when you walked out this morning in leather pants."

"I have *not* renounced anything, *Ranger* Foster." Roxanne laughed and pushed his shoulder playfully. "I just figured I worked so hard wrapping them it would be nice to make sure they got delivered on time."

She shrugged into the coat, flipped her hair free of the hood, and winked at him as he pulled his own parka over his arms. "And, by the way, I'm pretty sure, like, ninety percent of twenty-something fashionistas have these exact leather pants on their wish list this year, too, just so you know. There may even be a pair in Santa's sleigh for you, *if* you're lucky."

"Well, in that case," Mark said, pulling the back door open and motioning to the landscape of snowy white outside. "I can't wait to see what Santa's got waiting for me under the tree tomorrow morning. Let's deliver some toys."

Chapter Twelve

Like chopping firewood and preparing homemade steak dinners, Roxanne had never been in a snowcat. "So it's like, a part-truck, part-tractor sort of thing?"

"Just think of it as a car for driving through snow."

The snowcat seemed weirdly powerful as it waited, engine purring, while Mark helped her climb up into the passenger seat and closed the door behind her. Big, square, and rumbling, it was by far the oddest vehicle she had ever ridden in.

From her position in the passenger bucket seat, Roxanne followed Mark with her gaze as he moved around the nose of the cab to the driver's side. She had thought her BMW had an excessive number of bells and whistles, and it did, but the cockpit of her car did not compare to the snowcat's, which had more pedals and levers than she could dream up uses for. Apparently, driving in the snow was complicated business. "I've never seen so many knobs and gauges in one vehicle before."

"I thought the same thing when I saw the dashboard of your car."

"Very funny."

The snowcat was larger and roomier inside than it appeared from the outside, with enough space in the floorboard of the front seat for Roxanne's luggage to sit comfortably and still leave plenty of room for her feet. A large center console and two long gearshifts separated the bucket seats, and Mark had neatly piled all the children's gifts into the cab's backseat. Underneath, rubber tracks wrapped over rubber wheels, which gave the entire machine an odd, rocking type of stance as Mark climbed into the driver's seat and buckled in. One of those pine-scented tree air fresheners hung from the rearview mirror, and an old AM/FM radio had been fitted into the dash. It only picked up two stations, both of which blasted carols.

"Which do you prefer, navigator?" Mark handed Roxanne two matching yellow legal pads as he adjusted various mirrors and turned on the defroster. He twisted the knobs on the old analog radio. "Classics?" he asked, pausing as Burl Ives's rich vibrato filled the cab, and then spun forward until a pop singer's smooth soprano warbled through the airwaves. "Or modern?"

"Your turn. I picked last time, remember?"

Mark shrugged. "You picked so well I thought I'd let you go again."

"Classics," Roxanne decided, thinking of Bogart. "They've been playing the pop stuff on repeat in the lobby of *Divine* since Thanksgiving. I might be okay with never hearing it again."

Mark nodded in agreement as he adjusted the dial back to Burl and lowered the volume so they could talk over the music. "Can't beat an old favorite."

Roxanne reviewed the notepads. "Nice penmanship, Santa. You've got quite the list here."

"Lots of good folks up in the mountains." He leaned over and ran a gloved finger down one of the pages. "This one's a list of names and ages, and the other"—he reached for the second list—"is an itemized inventory of everything we wrapped."

The lists were long, but not overwhelming, and Roxanne knew her way around a good inventory. "All right, Santa. So what's the plan?"

Mark pulled a lever, adjusted a knob, and shifted out of neutral. The snowcat purred gratefully as it lurched into the snow, crunching powder under its tracks when it crawled forward confidently. "I'll drive the sleigh if you take care of the lists." He winked at her and smiled. "Make sure to check them twice."

For the next several hours, they moved through the snow, visiting small homes and delivering gifts Mark carefully selected from the stash in the backseat. They made a great team. Mark would recite the address of each home as they arrived, and Roxanne would give the names and ages of the children from the first list. He'd pick up, shake, and ponder over several gifts before choosing the right one, and she'd strike the corresponding number from her second list as Mark slipped out of the cab and jogged to the front door with his selections in hand. He took his time choosing the perfect gift for each child on his list, but Roxanne didn't complain. It made the time go by more slowly, and she was in no hurry.

"Do you know all of these people personally?" she asked after he'd spent a particularly long time at one of the houses, chatting with an elderly woman who had tried on numerous occasions to pull him inside.

"Not all of them."

Roxanne wasn't sure she believed him. "Sure seems like you do. I haven't seen you go up to a door yet where someone didn't pull you in for hugs and handshakes."

"People are just friendly up this way."

Friendly? Roxanne raised an eyebrow. "I'll say. You've got enough baked goods to go into hibernation. I saw the blanket, too—and the candy cane ornament."

Mark gave a noncommittal shrug. "I didn't bring anything back from the last house."

"You hid the gifts under the front door mat and ran back to the snowcat before anyone could see you! You wouldn't even turn the radio back up until we were halfway down the street."

"Yeah." Mark winked. "But no gifts."

Roxanne rolled her eyes and held back a laugh. "I'm not sure that counts."

Mark's enthusiasm for his role as Santa was infectious, and sometime between the first house and the fifteenth, Roxanne was singing along with the radio and enjoying picking out the perfect gifts as much as he was. In fact, she'd almost completely forgotten she was due back at her family's cabin or that Hunter hadn't bothered to check on her after her trip. She'd stopped checking the time around the time they'd unwrapped one of the pies—a cinnamon apple crisp—and dug in with two plastic forks Mark pulled from the glove compartment. While not as delicious as the maple pie, it was still amazing.

When at last they pulled into the long stretch of gravel that marked the entrance to the final house on their list, Mark crept slowly up the drive and killed the engine. "Come with me on this one."

"Oh, I don't think I should." Roxanne's pulse rose in her throat. "I don't know these people."

"Even better." Mark picked up the last three gifts that remained on the backseat and laid them in her arms. "Giving gifts to strangers accounts for half the fun, at least."

He slipped out of his seat and shut the door behind him before Roxanne could conjure up a believable reason why she shouldn't help. She was still objecting when he opened her door and reached for her hand. Clutching the presents against her chest, she slipped her glove into his and bit her lip, allowing herself to be led out of the snowcat.

"Don't be shy," Mark teased, helping her down the guardrails. "They don't bite. I promise."

She sank one foot into ankle-deep white. "It's not biting I'm worried about, it's—"

Roxanne was still saying something about feeling weird delivering presents to people she didn't know when her left foot slipped on a patch of ice.

It happened faster than she could have expected. First, she was looking at the trees and ground blanketed in peaceful white calm, and then she was pinned against Mark's chest, clinging to his jacket as she struggled to regain her footing. The presents tumbled unceremoniously into the snow, thudding as they fell, but he held her easily, his right arm around the small of her back and his left hand on her elbow, gripping her tightly.

"I've got you."

Mark's voice was soft and reassuring, but there was a hint of something unsaid in his words as Roxanne tilted her head to his. It was suddenly so warm—hot even. The wintry weather might as well have been replaced by a summer heat wave as Roxanne stared into the deep green of the ranger's eyes.

Mark's lips were inches from hers, and she wanted to taste them more than all the pies tempting her waistline in the cab of the snowcat. She could feel his arms tightening around her, the hand formerly on her elbow joining his other where it wrapped around her back. Her eyelids fluttered shut as Mark lifted her against him, closing the distance between their bodies through the soft press of their thick winter coats. Roxanne felt the tickle of his breath against her lips.

"It's Ranger Mark!" The shrill sound of a child's voice called out across the snow, ending the moment.

Roxanne's eyes flew open.

"Hey, Mikey and Clara, Ranger Mark is here!"

This announcement was followed by a front door banging against the wall and the patter of several pairs of little feet pounding across the snow. Roxanne pretended to brush a lock of hair out of her eyes as she hid the blush in her cheeks from Mark and averted her gaze, anchoring her feet in the slippery patch of ice so she could safely release her grip on his coat and peel her body away from his. He cleared his throat and unwound his arms, then bent to retrieve the presents strewn across the snowy ground.

"Okay, I might have fibbed," he joked, eyeing the small herd of children rushing toward them. "Sometimes the little one does bite."

Roxanne laughed, but she still sized up the kids. It was hard to distinguish which was the littlest under the bulk of their heavy winter coats.

By the time he made it back to his feet, the sweet tension building between them had dissipated. Mark hooked his right palm on Roxanne's elbow as they moved in the direction of the children trudging their way toward them over the snow-capped lawn.

"Hey, Costas!" he called, waving at the children. The Costas waved six sets of hands back.

Roxanne smiled as politely as she could as the kids closed in around them. "I'm not very good with kids," she admitted. "I don't think I've ever even hugged my niece and nephew."

Actually, she'd never spent much time around children at all, except for the occasional few who appeared on the set of a photo shoot in her building. Even then, they were generally sticky and prone to tantrums, and they had a habit of making Roxanne very, very uncomfortable.

"It's not that I don't *like* kids," she felt compelled to clarify. "I'm just ... mildly frightened of them."

"You're in luck." Mark smirked. "You've got a ranger with you. Follow my lead."

Unnatural stiffness locked Roxanne's body in place as the three children arrived in front of them.

"Roxy, this is Charlie and Mikey." Mark put a hand atop each boy's head. "And this is Clara."

Clara, the youngest and probable biter, had run up with her brothers but hid her face shyly behind a ragged baby doll when she gazed up at Mark with a look of obvious adoration. She was holding a sprig of something green in her hand, but quickly hid it in her pocket. Naturally, Mark pretended not to notice his youngest fan's ardor and, after handing off the presents to her brothers, swept her up in his arms.

"I think you've gotten prettier since the last time I saw you, Clara Costa," he cooed, which made the pink in her cheeks turn scarlet. "Santa left this at my house by mistake"—he handed her a small, lumpy package from inside his coat—"but I think it was meant for you."

Her face lit up. The little girl tore off the wrapping paper to expose a doll with twin strawberry braids and a gingham dress. Clara grinned at Mark and squeezed her arms around his neck, her eyes falling on Roxanne as she laid her head in the hollow of Mark's shoulder.

"Who's she?" Clara's voice was tight with the thinly veiled jealousy of a little girl in love.

Mark turned his back on the boys so he and Clara could face Roxanne, shivering more from nerves than cold in her borrowed winter gear. "That," he said, winking conspiratorially at Roxanne, "is my friend Roxy."

Clara looked skeptical as Roxanne attempted a casual wave.

"She lives in New York City." The skepticism in the little girl's eyes sharpened immediately into interest. "And she works for a big fashion magazine with lots of beautiful people. She's *very* smart. I bet if you ask her really nicely, she'll help you pick out a name for your new friend."

Clara wriggled out of Mark's arms and sped to Roxanne, thrusting the new doll in her hands. Roxanne gave a panicked look to Mark, who nodded at her encouragingly.

"Hi, Clara." Her voice cracked on the little girl's name. She cleared her throat and tried again. "I used to have a doll like yours.

I sewed it a dress similar to this one."

Clara was now looking up at her with the same sort of admiration she'd given the ranger, and it made Roxanne's insides feel like jelly. Suddenly, more than anything, she wanted to deserve it. She wasn't sure if anyone had ever looked at her that way before, and she felt so weirdly maternal she almost reached out and hugged the little girl. If Spencer had seen her like this, he'd have teased her mercilessly—*forever*. She'd almost forgotten about her dolls and their homemade dresses. Those had been her earliest designs.

"What should we name her?" Clara asked, grinning mischievously as if this were a task of great importance, which of course it was.

Roxanne studied the doll. Its ginger braids and old-time dress reminded her of *Anne of Green Gables*, as did Clara's slightly crooked smile. "How about Anne?" she suggested, handing the doll back to Clara.

She watched as the little girl pondered the name.

"I like it," she decided.

"I do, too," Roxanne agreed. "It's nice to meet you, Anne," she directed to the doll.

"Welcome home, Anne," Mark added.

Roxanne looked at the house and saw the front door had opened again. A willowy woman wrapped in a thick shawl stood in the doorway, watching the goings-on with a smile. Without thinking about it, Roxanne waved. The woman smiled and waved back.

Mark had been right: delivering a gift to a stranger was fun.

Clara hugged the doll against her chest, and something cold whizzed past Roxanne's head. Then another. A third hit Mark square in the back and Clare wrapped her small body around Roxanne's waist as Mark spun in front them, his arms spread wide in a defensive posture.

"It's an attack," he yelled in an exaggerated, playful voice. "Quick! Get behind me, girls. I'll protect you."

No sooner had he finished his vow than another pair of snowballs flew over a makeshift dune in the snow. One hit Mark in the arm, the other in the leg. Roxanne squealed and pulled Clara behind her. Together they ducked behind Mark as he scooped up a palmful of snow and prepared to return fire.

Twenty minutes and dozens of snowballs later, everyone was caked in half-melted snow. Roxanne had initially hidden behind Mark, then the snowcat, but when Clara had tossed her doll down in the white dunes and made miniature balls of her own, Roxanne had been moved into battle as well. At first, it was hard to tell who was winning, but the speed and tirelessness of the twins had been edging above Mark and the girls.

At the moment, Mark had his hands on his knees and was pleading for mercy while the boys hid behind their dune, either making more ammunition or deliberating the ranger's surrender—it was impossible to know which.

Roxanne saw her opening to turn the tables. She gathered up her snowballs and Clara's into the curve of her arm. The twins had been banking on Mark as their most dominant opponent and had underestimated the woman behind the snowcat. If she could run up in front of Mark, she could pelt the boys with handfuls at once, then scurry onto the front porch and slip behind a rocking chair which had been designated as neutral territory after the kids' mom had offered a supportive wave and closed the front door.

Her plan was good, but her timing was off, and the crunching sounds of her leather pants gave her away. No sooner had she emerged from behind the open passenger-side door of the snowcat than the tops of the boys' heads appeared behind the curve of the snowbank. She saw that they had not been considering Mark's surrender after all but had been busy rolling a snowball the size of a snowman's belly, which they had loaded into a slingshot fashioned from one of their scarves. Each had taken one end of the scarf and was preparing for launch.

The next few seconds passed in slow motion. Roxanne saw the fatal missile but was carried forth by her own momentum.

"Roxy, look out!" Clara yelled in warning.

Mark turned, diving in front of Roxanne. The giant snowball hit him in the stomach, slamming him into Roxanne and throwing the pair into a tangled heap of arms and legs on the snow.

It took them both a minute to catch their breath, but when they did, Roxanne was hyperaware of the way Mark felt on top of her. The boys were cheering somewhere nearby, and Clara ran up to stand over them, giggling.

"My hero," Roxanne whispered, the volume of her voice cut in half from the fall and the faraway sensation she felt under the weight of Mark's body.

Whatever Mark was saying back was lost inside a heavy exhale of breath, but it sounded like he was torn between a "you're welcome" and an apology. One of his hands was wedged against the side of her cheek, and she felt its heat despite the icy glove.

In her peripheral vision, Roxanne saw Clara hovering above them, holding something in her hand. It was green with white berries, tied in a red bow. Roxanne realized with a heart thump the little girl was holding a sprig of mistletoe. It was crumpled from where she had retrieved it from her pocket, but still clinging dearly to life and looking decidedly impish for a plant. Clara held it above their heads, but the doll in the gingham dress did the talking for her.

"You have to kiss her now," Clara mumbled in a sweet ventriloquist's voice, bobbing Anne the Doll around in the air with her other hand.

From his position above her, Mark looked at Roxanne, his brows furrowed in an expression which plainly said he did not know how to proceed. It was the first time she'd seen the capable ranger lost for words, and at no point in the past couple of days they'd spent together had he looked so completely irresistible.

"I told you they didn't bite, but I didn't know they had other tricks up their sleeves."

"It *is* mistletoe," Roxanne managed to whisper around the lump in her throat.

The tension in Mark's eyebrows loosened and his thumb brushed across her cheek as he lowered his face to hers.

"It is mistletoe."

This time when Roxanne heard the sound of sleigh bells, they were clear and distinct, and Mark pressed his lips against hers.

Chapter Thirteen

Even though they were lying in ice, Roxanne was pretty sure her body was on fire. When Mark finally pulled his lips away from hers, the heat of his kiss had all but melted her into the snow. What she was completely certain of, however, was she had never been kissed like that before. It had been a tender, chaste, mistletoe-appropriate kiss, which somehow made it even more intoxicating.

She felt it all the way in her toes.

Clara squealed and the boys made exaggerated gagging noises, but Roxanne hardly heard any of it as Mark pushed himself to his feet and helped her up beside him. It was impossible not to stare at him, but Roxanne did her best to pretend one simple kiss hadn't rocked her entire world.

You should feel guilty, she scolded herself. Mistletoe or not, she had no business kissing someone who was barely more than a stranger, especially not when she still had an ex-boyfriend to deal with and not when she was about to say goodbye to Ranger Mark Foster forever. Thanks to his hospitality and unwavering holiday cheer, she'd fallen victim to the draw of the spirit over the past day.

But the thought of Mark walking out of her life in a matter of hours? That would make this the most heartbreaking holiday ever. Her Grinch status was about to go up another notch, her heart shrink one more size. She might even go so far as to entertain the thought of wearing green, which was totally *not* her color.

But all that could wait. Roxanne was so lost in the aftershock of her impromptu mistletoe kiss that she only barely moved through the motions of saying goodbye to the Costa kids. Their mother had appeared again in the doorway with thank-yous, hugging first Mark and then Roxanne before they climbed back into the snowcat and began the last leg of their trek toward the Hudson family cabin.

The blue winter sky was quickly turning purple, and it would be twilight soon. Everyone was starting to tuck in for a long winter's night—except Roxanne. There was a hollow feeling growing in her stomach, and it got a bit bigger with every crunch of the wheels on the uneven snowy ground. She no longer had the energy to sing along with the radio, and was entirely aware she was pouting, though she couldn't summon the will to do anything about it.

Humbug, she felt like saying, but didn't.

"Everything okay?" Mark's voice filled the silence that had been hanging in the cab since they'd left the Costa homestead. He turned down the volume on the radio so listening to music could no longer be a handy excuse. The snowcat became quiet as he peered at her out of the corner of his eye.

"Yes, of course." Roxanne shook her head and offered him a smile, waiting a little too long to answer. "I'm surprised we got done with delivering all of those presents so quickly. I think it took longer to wrap them all than it did to hand them out."

Mark laughed, letting her off the hook. "Tell me about it. It was great seeing all those kids, though. Best part of my Christmas Eve for sure."

"Plus you've got enough pie to keep you full on sweets till Valentine's Day," Roxanne noted, surveying the bakery that had taken up residence in the backseat of the snowcat.

"That I do." Elvis Presley's "Blue Christmas" had come on the radio, and Mark tapped his fingers to the crooner's beat on the steering wheel.

Roxanne smiled politely but wasn't sure what to say next.

"There are a few maple pies back there," Mark said. "You should take one, or three. You earned them."

Just the thought of the rich, creamy dessert made Roxanne's stomach growl with anticipation. She patted her stomach quiet.

"I'll have to pass," she said sadly, trying not to think of the sweet flavor of maple pie.

"How come? And don't say it's because you don't have a sweet tooth, because I won't believe you."

Laughing, Roxanne slapped lightly at his arm. "Oh, I've got the sweet tooth. I could eat pie for breakfast, lunch, and dinner, no problem. But it will be time to tuck into summer fashion when I get back to *Divine*, and summer means one thing—bathing suit season is coming."

Mark cocked his eyebrows, not seeing the connection. "Isn't it kind of early to be thinking about swimwear? Everything outside is a solid field of white."

"True. But the world of fashion has one speed—light speed—and it doesn't pause for holidays once retail moves on to the next big season. Designers are already sending in samples of their summer fashions. Want a sneak peek? It's spandex."

The last was a tease—she hoped. Most fabrics had a way of coming back into style, but Spandex was one she hoped the entire fashion industry would unanimously agree should not.

Mark winced playfully. "Thanks for the warning." A beat passed. "But bathing suit season doesn't mean you can't have pie. You can even eat pie while wearing a bathing suit, or so I've heard."

He did have a point.

"I could, but I'd love to see you sell the idea of a pie-friendly diet into the fashion industry. Everyone's watching what they eat, all the time. Even the people who just write about it." She pointed both of her thumbs backward at herself and shrugged.

"Now, I'm a lowly mountain man, and I don't mean to be rude, but isn't fashion supposed to make people feel *more* beautiful, not less?"

Again, Roxanne found it hard to argue Mark's point. "You'd think so, wouldn't you? Body shaming is definitely out, but the industry's definition of beautiful hasn't quite caught up—at least, not in high fashion. The needle has moved, no pun intended, but barely." She thought again of Andrea Steiner, the lovely young model who had all the symptoms of an eating disorder.

"Beauty shouldn't be something that comes with a dress size or how well you can accessorize," she found herself saying, her voice growing more impassioned with every word as she gave voice to words she'd only ever thought before and had never shared with anyone—certainly not Hunter, or Spencer. "Everyone deserves to feel beautiful in their own skin, not because of the labels they're wearing. That's what I want—fashion that's flattering even, or maybe *because*, you had pie for breakfast. I want people to feel beautiful, not constantly worry about whether they look it or not."

"Sounds like you're the person to change things then."

"I hope so." Roxanne's passion deflated as she remembered Vivian still hadn't gotten back to her on the sketches she'd shared—or, if she had, her message was stuck in cyberspace, waiting to make its way into her inbox. She pulled her cell phone from her coat pocket, surprise rising goosebumps on her skin when she saw full bars and a screen full of notifications. There were a few unread messages from Spencer, and another, surprisingly, from Hunter, and her inbox count had risen. She decided to ignore them all for the moment—it would be rude to get glued to her phone mid-conversation—and pushed the phone back into her pocket with a sigh. "One day. But right now I can't get people to take my designs seriously, much less my ideas."

"They will."

The way Mark said it was so matter-of-fact Roxanne actually dared to believe him.

"In that case," she said, the promise of the sweet custard already tantalizing her taste buds. "I think I'll take a pie. I might take two."

Mark laughed but didn't say anything. Instead, he pointed to a clearing up ahead, and when Roxanne looked up, she recognized the landscape immediately, though it had been years since she'd last seen it and night was quickly falling, blanketing the scene in darkness. At the edge of an unmarked street was a large hemlock tree she'd loved to climb as a girl. Beyond was the long driveway serving as the entrance to the private road that led to her family's cabin.

Her father's truck would be parked out front, where he always liked to leave it, and there would be piles of seasoned firewood on the porch. Even at the slow pace of the snowcat, they'd be there in less than five minutes. Already Roxanne could see the evidence of chimney smoke unfurling in the air and telltale tire tracks on an otherwise unblemished road, denoting the other cars that were parked ahead.

"Hey," Roxanne started, but then she had to pause to take a breath. Though she'd just been fired up, she suddenly felt chilled, and her pulse had started to race. "Listen, I was thinking. I want to thank you for everything you've done for me. Pulling me out of the snow, taking me in, today, the pie—everything. Would you like to come to Christmas dinner tomorrow night with my family?"

When he didn't answer right away, Roxanne's stomach clenched. "Not, like, a date or anything. Just … a thank you. For everything. I promise there'll be more than pie, and I won't be the one cooking," she added, pitifully. "I totally understand if you have other plans"—which she knew he didn't, since he'd told her as much—"but I'd love it if you came."

Mark pursed his lips as if in thought and answered as the cabin finally came into view. "I would love to."

There was hesitancy in his voice, and embarrassment crawled up Roxanne's throat as she wondered if she'd misread things.

"But I'd hate to interrupt a family holiday," he continued. "Maybe you should talk it over with your folks first, and—"

"Trust me, they won't mind at all." Roxanne was relieved his hesitancy was out of consideration for her family, and not a rejection of her. She probably should have asked her parents before inviting over the ranger for their holiday dinner, but it wasn't like they'd have said no. After all, if nothing else, Mark had *literally* rescued her from becoming a human popsicle during a blizzard. "I'm sure my parents would be more than happy to have you join us. I wouldn't be here at all if weren't for you."

Besides, she was pretty sure she was allowed a plus one. Rachel had brought home a different guy every year before she'd gotten married, and no one had said a word. Roxanne had barely come home herself, much less brought a date, so she was pretty sure no one would mind. She'd never invited Hunter to come with her the few times she'd visited her family, though he was drop-dead gorgeous and would have made her sister's head spin with envy.

Inviting Mark to Christmas dinner is not a date. It was a thank you, and *just* a thank you. And he wasn't a stranger, either. Her dad had spoken to him in a familiar manner on the radio. He probably knew Mark better than she did.

"Well, in that case, count me in." Mark brought the snowcat to a full stop a few yards from the cabin's long front porch. He didn't turn off the engine this time, but he dimmed the headlights and slipped on his gloves before opening the driver's side door. He pushed it open, clicked on a flashlight to help him see in the deepening twilight. The look he gave her when he turned back let her know he was serious about what he'd say next. "Thank you for the invite, Roxy, really. I'd love to join you for dinner." He grinned. "I'll bring some bourbon to go with all the pies you're confiscating."

He winked at her, and she laughed at his back as he slid out of the snowcat. His boots landed heavily in the snow.

"Deal."

Roxanne waited for Mark to pull open her door and allowed

herself to be helped out of the passenger side, along with her purse and a pie in each of her hands. She'd gotten pretty comfortable with falling in the snow but didn't want to damage her precious cargo. Mark put the flashlight between his teeth as he held her elbow with one hand. It took her a moment, again, to get her footing, and he graciously gave her time, then grabbed the handle of her suitcase with the other. When he had everything situated, he used his shoulder to push the door shut, and made sure she was steady before palming the flashlight. He returned a few anchoring fingers to her forearm in case she needed a quick rescue from the snowy terrain.

"All set?" His flashlight was aimed at their feet.

"Yep," Roxanne confirmed, though what she wanted to say was *forget this; let's go back to your place.* Several similar sentiments were competing for her voice, so she decided not to attempt to say anything else and trudged quietly through the snow, Mark at her side. She felt a different sensation when he touched her now. Did he feel the same way?

Get your head together. Roxanne was about to see her family for the first time in years, and showing up covered in still-melting snow and carrying pie was not how she'd imagined the reunion. Nor had she expected to be lost in thought, mooning over a forest ranger who didn't know flannel from Fendi.

She was Roxanne Hudson, up-and-coming fashion editor at *Divine*, for Pete's sake! Model dater, jetsetter, Milan Fashion Week veteran. Women like Roxanne did not get weak-kneed over a simple kiss with some random rugged mountain man—not even if they were as sweet and genuine and annoyingly perfect as Mark Foster. In two days, she'd be back in the City and life would go on as it had all along. The past day-and-a-half would be chalked up to holiday sugar highs and bourbon. She'd probably never even tell Spencer about Mark.

As they neared the cabin, Mark's flashlight became unnecessary, thanks to the warm glow of the lights decorating the outside of the cabin and the huge, ornamented fir tree standing inside the front picture window. Roxanne's initial assessment had been right: At least from the outside, the scene *was* very Currier and Ives, and not so much Martha and Snoop Dogg.

Her father, always a holiday decoration enthusiast, and her mother, an interior designer, had spared no detail in equipping the cabin's exterior to be everything Grandma Myrtle might have wanted for her last Christmas. Red velveteen ribbon and frosted light bulbs were wrapped around any fixture that did not move. Icicle lights clung to the edges of the cabin's eaves, dotted with circular red bulbs that looked like holly berries. Ivy garland made the cabin green and alive amidst the ice and snow.

A large fake snowman stood beside the picture window as if wishing to be invited indoors to gaze upon the massive fir tree, decked with so much garland and ornamentation it appeared every branch of the tree had been gilded with holiday cheer. It was hard not to feel warm, standing outside in the snowy cold, when presented with such a heartwarming view.

Mark pressed his fingers lightly into Roxanne's arm, and his voice rumbled down to her as they closed the distance between the snowcat and the cabin. "Your folks really outdid themselves. I haven't seen the place this decked out in years. It looks fantastic."

"Yeah," Roxanne mused, all her troubles momentarily forgotten. "It's beautiful."

The pair climbed up to a small stairway to the porch landing and stopped at the welcome mat—the same one that had sat on the front porch this time of year since she'd been a girl: a coconut-fiber rectangle featuring an image of Santa in his sleigh, presents piled high. As they paused at the door and Mark settled her luggage at her side, Roxanne saw the spray of mistletoe hanging above their heads.

A heavy puff of smoke filled the air between them as she exhaled. "I guess this is it."

Mark peered down at her, and Roxanne was surprised to find he was standing so close she could see the reflections of the lights strung along the eaves in his eyes. She heard the rustling sound of his coat as he slid the flashlight into his pocket. One of his hands closed around the bend of her elbow, and he began to draw her toward him.

"I'm just glad I could get you home in time for the holiday." A playful smile flitted across his lips.

Roxanne resisted the urge to roll her eyes, but a laugh slipped out anyway. "Well, I couldn't miss Christmas." She jerked her head toward the door and her family on the other side. She took a step closer, so Mark's coat pressed against hers. "They'd never let me live it down."

"Aw, come on," he breathed as his other hand slid around her waist. "I think you're starting to like this time of year a little bit more than you're letting on."

Roxanne summoned her courage. "I do like the mistletoe." She bit her lip, hoping the sting of her teeth would help her keep from giggling. She hadn't felt this good standing on her parents' front porch with a boy in a *long* time.

"You know, I'm normally not a big fan, but I have to admit there is something different about it this year." He'd taken her hint and was pulling her in, locked in his arms under the mistletoe for the second time that day.

She was still watching Mark's lips move as he bent his head toward hers when the sound of the front door opening caught her attention. As the two abruptly released each other, a whiff of cologne so expensive you could almost smell the price tag flooded Roxanne's senses. When she looked up, it wasn't her father or brother-in-law welcoming her home—it was Hunter.

Chapter Fourteen

Hunter, who was supposed to be in Madrid, was instead standing in the doorframe of Roxanne's family's cabin. Whether he'd just gotten there or was preparing to leave, she couldn't begin to guess, because Hunter was always dressed like he was coming or going, and never like he was happy to be standing still in one place. Even his body was a thing of constant motion— his knees always slightly bent and his hair moving of its own accord regardless of whether there was a breeze or not.

Whichever direction he was headed, Hunter was flawless as usual, in dark denim jeans and leather boots. Perfectly color-coordinated layers clung to his shoulders and torso like they'd been made for his body, which they probably had. Wisps of artfully arranged hair flared out of the rim of his knit cap, and his face was covered in the kind of five o'clock shadow that took a few days and careful trimming to achieve.

No one would ever look at Hunter Hollister and say he was anything other than perfect, but right now, at this second, he was the last person Roxanne wanted to see.

"Hunter?" She felt dumb stating the obvious but was not quite sure she believed her eyes. It was completely impossible Hunter would be standing right in front of her. "What are you doing here? I thought you weren't going to make it home in time for Christmas."

If he'd guessed she was about to kiss the strapping ranger standing beside her under the mistletoe, he didn't show it. Everything about his expression was smooth, cool, and utterly devoid of emotion—the picture-perfect mask of someone trained to smile. When his eyes finally landed on hers, Roxanne couldn't decode them, and they'd been dating off and on for nearly four years.

He smiled, flashing brilliantly white teeth so bright they rivaled the snow, and spread his hands out wide in greeting. "Surprise, babe. Managed to get a flight home last minute. You think I'd miss spending the holidays with my girlfriend?"

The emphasis on the word "girlfriend" was blatant, and Roxanne felt Mark go rigid at her side.

"You mean *ex*-girlfriend," she clarified. "We broke up, remember?"

Hunter cocked an eyebrow but said nothing as the tension mounting on the porch hiked higher. Finally, Mark cleared his throat and extended his hand. It was one of those automatic gestures men did, at least the ones raised on old-fashioned manners, as she'd presumed Mark was. Hunter could have been a king cobra rising up in front of them, and the ranger might still have tried to play nice and get along.

"Mark Foster. Green Mountain Patrol." His voice sounded tight, and he wasn't smiling. He hadn't moved when Roxanne had pulled away from him, but he had somehow managed to edge

115

himself in front of her, positioning himself between her and the man in the doorway. Depending on one's perception, it might have been protectiveness or possessiveness. It might have even been a little of both, or neither.

Hunter let Mark's outstretched hand hang a heartbeat too long before he accepted it with a gracious smile, the face of the pricy TAG Heuer watch on his wrist flashing under the lights. "Hunter Hollister. Thank you so much for helping Roxanne get home, Ranger."

He dropped Mark's hand and turned his gaze to her. "Let's get you in and cleaned up, babe. Your mother has been brewing a pot of wassail all day and everyone's waiting." He gave her outfit an appraising look as if noticing it for the first time. When his eyes got to the fluffy parka, his nose crinkled. "What are you wearing? Thank God no one had to see you like this."

"Oh." Roxanne blinked rapidly a few times, remembering she was still wearing Mark's sister's things, and reached up to unzip her borrowed winter parka. "I completely forgot. You'll want to get this back to Maggie."

His hand free of Hunter's, Mark moved to stay her hand with his and stopped just short of touching her. "Don't worry about it," he croaked in his still-tight voice. "You might need a better coat. I can pick it up another time."

Roxanne heard the message hidden inside Mark's words and had a hard time meeting his gaze. "You're still coming tomorrow for dinner, right?" She knew it was a bad idea to push the invitation, but she wasn't able to help herself from asking. Things were suddenly moving too fast. She heard the sound of sleigh bells in her ears again, but this time they sounded far away and sad.

"Actually ..." Mark's voice waned as he avoided eye contact and his smile didn't reach his eyes. "Perhaps it's not a great idea. It seems like you've got a full house already, and I hate to be a bother. The invite was more than enough of a thanks, really."

Roxanne's stomach lurched, swallowing what was left of her Grinchy heart. She knew rejection when she encountered it and felt herself go into self-preservation mode. She inhaled and put on a smile so practiced and cool it made Hunter's version look amateurish. Spencer would have been proud of the way she pushed one side of her mouth a little higher than the other, so her face morphed instantly from optimistic to unimpressed. Her righted posture earned her another three inches of height, all of them ice. It wasn't only her writing skills that had helped her up the rungs of *Divine*—Roxanne knew how to play the game as well as the best.

When he looked up and saw the expression on Roxanne's face, Mark's smile faltered. He blinked a few times, then pulled a business card out of his coat pocket, and Roxanne plucked it carefully from his fingertips. The tips of their gloves didn't even get a chance to touch. She arched her eyebrows in an unspoken question.

"Henry over at Henry Hauls owes me a favor," Mark explained. "Give him a shout when you're ready for your car. He's expecting your call."

Roxanne swallowed heavily and forced her voice to remain aloof when it slid between her lips. "Thanks."

"Thanks for helping me deliver the toys. It was nice to have company."

She didn't know what to say to that, so she jerked her head in a quick nod and looked away.

Mark followed suit, but even with his head bowed she could see how his eyebrows furrowed. He opened his mouth as if to say something but decided against it. When he finally looked up, he was wearing his own version of a polished smile, but he wasn't as good at it as she was, and his voice gave him away. "Have a Merry Christmas, Roxy." With one last sideways nod at Hunter, Mark turned and walked out into the night, toward the snowcat.

Hunter snaked an arm around Roxanne's waist. She fought the urge to recoil. His touch was stiffer than Mark's had been, but familiar.

"Roxy?" The disdain was obvious in his voice. "No one calls you *Roxy*. Who is that guy, anyway—Ranger who?"

Roxanne watched Mark as he stepped into the snowcat and closed the door behind him. "No one. Just the guy who helped me get home." She didn't want to share the past forty-eight hours with Hunter, and she didn't want her thoughts to wander away with Mark as she allowed herself to be pulled into the cabin, watching over her shoulder as the no one who had become everything disappeared into the frozen darkness of Christmas Eve.

Chapter Fifteen

Regardless of how perturbed she was by his sudden appearance, Hunter was ever the gracious host as he shepherded Roxanne past her fawning relatives, both waving away her family with assurances they'd be right back with stories about Madrid and Roxanne's snowbound adventure.

"Hi, Mom." Roxanne tried to break away from Hunter's grip, but he kept moving, pulling her along in his wake.

"We'll be right back," he promised on their behalf in his best showman's voice. "Rox needs a few moments to freshen up and collect her breath. We're not used to this much snow in the City."

He walked behind her with one hand placed tenderly on her lower back and the other steering her by her upper arm. Anyone looking would have thought they were madly in love, but it was all an act they'd perfected after spending years evading the cameras at fashion shows and haute parties.

"You're a mess," he mumbled so only Roxanne would hear him. "You don't want to make an appearance looking like *that*."

It was the choreography of people escaping other people, although Roxanne and Hunter had vastly different reasons for doing so. Roxanne was not looking forward to the inevitable deluge of questions when she and Hunter were tucked privately away behind closed doors. The last they'd spoken, Hunter had suggested he needed to talk about their relationship. She had been sure he'd been rehearsing for his final stage exit, but the delicate way he was handling her made her second-guess herself.

What was he doing here? Roxanne thought back to their last conversation. She'd offered to text the address to her parents' cabin, but she hadn't—had she?

No, she decided. She definitely had not.

They didn't speak to each other as they made their way to the back bedroom which had been Roxanne's when she'd been a child. Instead, Roxanne pulled her suitcase along behind her and distracted herself by letting her thoughts run through the contents of her luggage, refusing to let her façade falter until she'd cached all remaining thoughts of Mark *and* decided on what to wear for the remainder of the evening. She'd over-packed, as usual, but at least she no longer had to worry about going out in the unrelenting cold.

Mercifully, Hunter was quiet behind her, and didn't ask any questions she didn't want to answer. It was a small Christmas miracle.

When they pushed into the bedroom at the end of the hall, Roxanne was surprised to find not much had changed in all the years since she'd stopped showing up for family holidays.

It looks just like it did before. Everything was as she'd left it: overwhelmingly pink, with paper dolls and back issues of assorted fashion magazines piled high along the cozy window seat that faced out on the western side of the cabin.

Spencer had been right, Roxanne thought. Being here *was* quaint, but it sure felt like home. She hadn't expected that.

"Seriously, what are you doing here? *How* did you even get here?" Roxanne asked Hunter when the door had closed behind them. "I didn't expect to see you till New Year." She felt like adding "or at all," but didn't.

"It's Christmas, the season of miracles," he answered, preoccupied with sorting through his luggage and laying items of clothing on the bed.

"I'm serious."

When he looked up and saw the glare Roxanne had leveled at him, Hunter blanched. "Vivian."

Roxanne's lips pinched into a straight line. She'd left the address with her boss in the event of an emergency, not to just hand over to anyone who asked for it. And Vivian wouldn't give it to anyone, that much was for sure. But then Hunter wasn't just anyone, was he? They'd been dating for years. Still, she couldn't imagine the woman would just hand over such personal information without asking, which would mean she'd have reached out to Roxanne first, right?

"When did you talk to Vivian?" she asked. The notification count on her inbox flashed in her memory. Was one of those unread emails about her designs?

"The other day." Hunter shrugged, deflecting, then fixed on an injured expression. "Is it really so bad I want to spend Christmas with my girlfriend?"

"First, we're broken up, if you didn't remember," Roxanne started, but before she could unleash, her father's deep baritone boomed down the hallway.

"Roxy, we're all waiting to hear about your drive in, c'mon girl," Robert Hudson called, which was code for *hurry up*.

Whatever she had to say to Hunter would have to wait, but that didn't mean she was going to let him off easy. "Christmas isn't just a holiday in the Hudson household," she snapped. "It's a semi-formal event. I hope you brought something to wear."

Hunter shot her a critical look. "I might say the same thing to you."

Roxanne's left eyebrow jerked upward so hard it hurt. "You know I was in a car accident, right? Two days ago. I think I look pretty good considering."

Hunter unzipped a cloth garment bag to reveal a length of rich red velvet. "I think you will look much better once you get into this."

She put her hand on her hip, determined not to be swayed by pretty clothing. Then Roxanne recognized the stepped neckline of the dress. The slight dip under the breast. The flare at the hem. She stared at the dress and realized it was one of the "Plain Jane" designs she'd drawn and handed a copy of to Vivian, but it was here. It was real.

"That's my dress."

"Yes, it is."

Her heart in her throat, Roxanne lifted the luxurious velvet and held it against her body, admiring the rich, shimmery quality of the fabric as it tumbled from her chest to the wooden floor at her feet. It was long but not heavy, with long sleeves and a wrap waist balanced by a thigh-high slit. She admired the delicate hand stitching and the slight tapering at the wrists. All the little details she'd drawn were there in her hands.

"I can't believe it. It's my dress. Hunter, it's … it's stunning. How did you get it?" She shifted her focus to Hunter to find he had already traded his dark jeans for black slacks and was watching her in the reflection of the room's dressing mirror as he buttoned up a collared shirt. His reflection rewarded her gaze with a satisfied smile, which could have just as easily been in response to her praise of the dress. It was hard to be sure with Hunter.

Hunter slipped a thin charcoal tie under his collar and worked it into an intricate Eldredge knot, then turned to her as he affixed a silver tie clip to complete the look. "A beautiful dress for a beautiful woman."

Another none answer, but this time Roxanne let it slide, still too caught up in the surprise of her dress. He gave her a small smile and tapped on the face of his watch in the universal signal to hurry up.

She did, excitedly pulling off the layers of borrowed, snow-crusted clothes, and sliding the dress up her legs and over her arms. "Help me zip up?"

Hunter pulled the dress's hidden zipper up her back in a cool breath of silky lining against her skin. He clasped the single pearl button at the nape of her neck. It fit like a glove, and Roxanne closed her eyes. She pulled in a deep breath and held it.

She felt Hunter's hands land on her shoulders and the soft press of his palms as he swiveled her to face him. When she opened her eyes again, she saw both of their reflections in the mirror, and the breath she had been holding caught in her throat. *Oh my gosh.* The dress had been beautiful on paper and striking on the bed, but on her body, it was more magnificent than she could have dreamed, clinging and flowing in all the right places as the color

123

caught the hazel of her eyes and brought out the flecks of gold. Maybe she had what it took to be a designer after all.

Behind her, Hunter was radiant, and even though she'd seen images of them side by side in more photographs than she could count, the combined effect of their holiday attire was astonishing. They truly were the kind of couple the camera loved—his skin light against her dark, complementary yet balanced—which went a long way in the world of fashion, regardless of whether or not it was real.

"So, what do you think?" he asked. "It's my favorite of your designs so far, and I thought you deserved to have it for your very own."

"I thought you said this dress was too ordinary," she said, recalling his former critique.

"I've reconsidered." Hunter swept her hair to the side and his eyes met Roxanne's in the mirror. His breath was as soft on her neck as the velvet on her skin. "I've actually had a chance to rethink a lot of things, Roxanne. Like us."

"I thought—" It was harder to say than she'd thought it would be. She swallowed and tried again. "When we broke up before you left, I thought it was for the last time. Then, a couple of days ago, you said you wanted to talk about our relationship, I was convinced it was—"

"What, over for good?" Hunter cut her off with an abrupt laugh as if the idea were preposterous. "I know things have been up and down lately, but I meant I wanted to talk about our relationship—to make it better. I don't want to lose you."

He laid a tender kiss in the dip of her shoulder, sending shivers down her skin. He nodded toward their reflection. "I want to get us back on track. We make the perfect couple, and I like how happy looks on us."

Roxanne placed her hand over his where it rested on her hip, but her smile didn't come easy. It wasn't easy to forget how she'd felt over the past few days, the stress of her job and everything else left behind. It had been so refreshing to just *be*, to not worry about ambitions and labels and what looked best on paper.

Still, as she considered their reflection, she was reminded of how hard she had worked for the life she had earned, and how—despite his flaws—Hunter had been there with her through it nearly every step of the way. Now, seeing her own design come to life, it was impossible to ignore the surge of pride as it moved through her body, straightening her posture and sweeping away the sentimentality that had begun to weigh down the edges of her thoughts.

It had been an interesting past few days, but at the end of it, Mark's maple pies and mistletoe kisses were in the past. Hunter, and her future, was still here.

Besides, which was more important? Following her dreams, or the sound of sleigh bells?

Chapter Sixteen

Roxanne held Hunter's arm as they returned to the family room, dispensing hugs and kisses all around. Everyone fawned over her dress, but Roxanne waved away the compliments, her cheeks heating from the attention. Hunter, meanwhile, preened for his audience.

"I'm sorry again for being so late," Roxanne said, smoothing the folds of her dress as she settled with Hunter on the overstuffed sofa.

"Don't think another minute about it, Roxy." Her dad dismissed the apology as Hunter reached over and took her hand. "We're just glad you made it in safely. Is your car damaged?"

"No," she answered, ignoring the look Hunter gave her out of the side of his eye. "Mark—Ranger Foster—said it looked completely fine. I wish I knew what happened. One minute, I was driving and the next, I was spinning. Mark said maybe it was Santa who ran me off the road."

Her family laughed, and her niece and nephew's eyes grew wide. "Santa?" they repeated. Their eager faces reminded Roxanne of the Costa kids, and she had a sudden craving for a snowball fight.

"That's right. He's coming tonight, you know," she told them, grinning.

"Roxanne doesn't have a reason to drive much in the City." Hunter cut in to change the subject. "She's too used to being chauffeured around. Besides, we couldn't resist a fashionably late entrance."

The remark made everyone laugh as he had intended … everyone except Roxanne and the kids.

"Tell us about everything, dear," Roxanne's mother encouraged her. "We're so glad you and Hunter could be here. We hadn't expected to see you both, and how nice to finally meet you, Hunter. What a wonderful Christmas surprise."

In the years since she'd seen them, her parents had gotten a little plumper, a little older, and, apparently, a lot happier. Retirement had been good to them, and she had never seen her mother smile so easily or heard her father laugh so hard. Ella and Ethan were bigger than she'd expected. Rachel was noticeably pregnant with a third bun in the oven, and although she knew the sex of the new babe, she wasn't sharing. Her husband, Ken, was his typical quiet self, the opposite of his wife, though his hair had started to thin a little, and there were new lines forming around his eyes that said parenthood hadn't been as easy as Rachel insisted it was.

Amidst them all, Grandma Myrtle sat in her wheelchair, smiling contentedly as she watched her family, her eyes sparkling with pride. Roxanne had hoped her parents' insistence this Christmas could be Grandma Myrtle's last might have been exaggerated—a conveniently timed ploy to pressure her into spending the wintery holiday with her family in the Green Mountain cabin instead of in her loft in the City—but she saw now it might be true. Grandma Myrtle had grown frail and fragile, her skin so papery it was nearly translucent and her hair the brittle texture of spun glass. Her eyes were clouded with cataracts, and her clothing hung off her shoulders like cloth flung over sticks.

"Grandma Myrtle," Roxanne said, drawing the old woman, who had remained quietly contemplative, into the conversation for the first time. "How are you feeling?"

"Oh, I'm doing all right, honey. Just ticking along, like always."

Myrtle's voice was as thin as her hair. Roxanne suddenly found smiling difficult.

"Your grandmother is in good spirits," Roxanne's father added, affecting a tender tone. "But it's good you were able to come home, Roxy."

Grandma Myrtle clicked her teeth at her son. "Don't worry my granddaughter, Robert. I'm fine."

There was a sharp pang in her chest Roxanne didn't quite recognize. It felt like sadness tinged with guilt. Grandma Myrtle had been such a big part of her life when she was growing up, but Roxanne hadn't bothered to even send a letter in over a year. Why was that? She'd sent a mail-order bouquet for Grandma Myrtle's last birthday. The office admin had ordered them on her behalf. Roxanne didn't even know what kind of flowers had been included.

Grandma Myrtle had once been Roxanne's biggest champion—the one who encouraged her to leave home to pursue her dreams. The one thing Myrtle had insisted on was for Roxanne to stay happy, and to always, *always* trust her heart. Despite her beautiful dress, her handsome companion, and her fancy byline, Roxanne was unsure if she'd succeeded.

"Did Ranger Foster take good care of you last night, Roxy?" her father asked.

"What?" Roxanne blinked, snapping out of her guilty reverie and into the present. Hunter squeezed her hand again—not in a reassuring kind of way, but in an impatient kind of way. He gave her a strange look she couldn't quite decipher. "Oh, yes. He was … he was a complete gentleman."

Her father nodded as if he'd assumed as much. "Mark Foster is a good man. One of the best rangers on the Green Mountain Patrol." He lifted a finger in the air in the way he did when he wanted to make sure you were listening. "Single-handedly organizes a toy drive for all the kids out in these parts whose families can't afford to give them a good Christmas. Collects the gifts, wraps them up, and spends Christmas Eve delivering them out. I expect that's what he's up to tonight."

"Actually, he delivered them already. I helped him wrap while we were snowed in. It took forever." Roxanne smiled, enjoying the memory. Her thoughts wandered back to the Costa kids. How would her family react to an impromptu snowball fight? Then she remembered the kiss under Clara's mistletoe and felt heat crawl up her cheeks. "He let me ride along with him in the snowcat, and we—"

"*You* spent the day delivering presents to needy kids? In a snowcat?" Hunter's voice was incredulous.

Roxanne's family stared at him, and he had the decency to look embarrassed. He cleared his throat and tried to save it.

"I mean to say, you spent the day roaming around with some forest ranger delivering presents to strangers instead of getting here as early as you could? Everyone has been waiting for you, including me. I was worried sick when I got here and heard you'd been in an accident."

The heat in Roxanne's cheeks turned into a different kind of fire. She wasn't sure whether to be insulted that Hunter would be so callous about her being charitable, or if she didn't like the way he'd spoken about Mark, or that he'd tried to make her feel guilty for being late to the cabin.

Actually, all of it was offensive. Especially considering he hadn't even had the decency to ask if she was okay after her accident.

She was about to say something to that effect when Grandma Myrtle cut in. "Giving back is good for the soul," she said matter-of-factly, bestowing upon Roxanne an approving smile as the family's inarguable matriarch. "Nothing brings out the real Christmas spirit like doing good for those around you. You did right, honey."

"Thank you, Grandma Myrtle. It felt right." Roxanne slid her hand out from under Hunter's, hoping he'd catch her point.

"It doesn't hurt that Mark Foster isn't hard on the eyes either," Rachel added. "I met him once when we brought the kids out during the summer, and *oh boy*." She giggled girlishly into her eggnog. She flipped her hand dismissively at Hunter, who was now busy looking insulted. "Not that you aren't handsome, Hunter. Don't mind me—baby hormones." She rubbed her belly and winked at Roxanne.

Roxanne put on her best diplomatic face and gave her sister a warning smile. "I didn't notice."

Rachel had always been boy crazy and an instigator, and Roxanne didn't want any drama with Hunter in front of her family. So far, he'd been oddly quiet about whatever he might have seen on the cabin's front porch, and Roxanne didn't want to tempt his jealousy when he was clearly on his best behavior—which in itself was something of a mystery. "Did Hunter tell you he's going to be premiering at London Fashion Week this year? He'll be working Armani," she said, trying to steer the conversation to safer topics for the man's ego.

While her family smiled good-naturedly, not having a clue what London Fashion Week was, Hunter played coy. "Oh, come on now, babe. No one cares about London Fashion Week right now. It's Christmas. Besides"—he gave the room a sly grin and smoothly turned the tables—"Roxanne hasn't told you her big news."

He turned to her encouragingly, but she had no idea what he was talking about. She pushed her breath out in a nervous laugh. "My news? I don't have any news."

Hunter put his hand dramatically to his head and sighed. "I assumed you knew already," he exclaimed, with staged effect, knowing perfectly well she hadn't had service to check her email, nor the opportunity to check her inbox before being rushed into the living room.

A tremor of excitement was running along Roxanne's nerves. "I haven't had cell reception. I saw a few new emails in my inbox when I got back in range, but I haven't had a chance to look at them."

And you know that, too, she thought.

He beamed, wrapping his arms around her, and directed the announcement at her family. "Roxanne shared some of her designs with Vivian Yurich, the editor in chief of *Divine*, who sent them to one of her dearest friends, Dahlia D'Arcy—*the* hottest up-and-coming couture designers in French fashion."

Roxanne's stomach hit the floor. She lifted her hand to stop him, but—

"And Dahlia *loved* them."

Roxanne's hand stalled in the air in front of her face. *What?*

"She loved them *so* much she's selected three of Rox's designs for her spring line and has asked Rox to join her at her firm in Paris." Hunter stood excitedly, pulling Roxanne on wobbling feet up beside him. "In fact, this dress is one of Roxanne's designs—not one of her latest, of course, but still a Roxanne Hudson original—freshly made by one of the premier tailors in Madrid. Doesn't she look absolutely stunning?"

Roxanne's family was congratulating her, but she couldn't hear it past the sound of her heart beating in her ears. She gawked at Hunter, all pretenses of posture completely forgotten in her shock. "Are you serious?" was all she could say. The room was spinning. She felt faint. It was everything she had hoped for—everything she had *dreamed* for—and now that it was happening, she couldn't believe it was real. She tried to sit back down, but Hunter held her upright, keeping her on her feet with her hands locked in his.

"Read your email, babe," Hunter grinned, exposing a row of perfect teeth. It was his real smile, the one that produced dimples on both sides of his mouth, and not the one he used for the camera. "You're the hottest piece of news right now, I promise you. Vivian

Yurich is already congratulating you on your move to France ... unless this isn't what you want?"

"It's what I've *always* wanted." The words felt hollow coming out of her lips, not because they were untrue, but because something had shifted in her, and they didn't fit completely right anymore. She really wanted to sit down, but Hunter hadn't loosened his grip on her hands and seemed intent on keeping her on her feet. Maybe she should have worn more comfortable shoes. It *was* fantastic news, but something about the way Hunter was sharing it made her uneasy, like she was missing the punchline of some elaborately planned joke. Like it was his big news and not hers. She resolved to phone Spencer the moment she could to verify the scoop. She should probably check her email, too.

"It's all part of what we've been working toward," Hunter pressed.

All Roxanne could do was smile, reflecting the expressions of each of her family members' faces. Only Grandma Myrtle seemed to recognize Roxanne's hesitation. Her clouded eyes looked stormy with concern.

Hunter took a deep breath and gave her hand a slight squeeze. She watched his Adam's apple bob in his throat as he swallowed. He stepped in closer to her so that the only place she could look was directly into his eyes.

"I have another surprise for you."

Hunter's his tone was suddenly hushed and conspiratorial. He released one of her hands and reached into his coat jacket, while simultaneously lowering himself down to one knee in front of her. Eyes still on hers, Hunter pulled a box from his pocket. Roxanne recognized the blue box and knew instantly what would be inside, even before she saw the black velvet of the box's interior. She heard a sharp intake of breath, but couldn't be sure if it was her mother's, or Rachel's, or maybe her own.

Roxanne's heart made the same sucking sound as the ring box as Hunter peeled it open. He had, of course, spared no expense—a ring like this was as much a reflection of him as it was of Roxanne. Flashing in the light of the tree, the world's most iconic engagement ring stared up at her. Four karats, flawless in a six-prong setting, the large center diamond floated above a brilliant Pavé band that twinkled as if it were made of stars. It was absolutely breathtaking, but when she looked at the ring Roxanne felt her blood run cold.

Too much, she thought. It's too much, too fast.

Hunter held the box open in front of her, allowing the dramatic tension to build in the room without saying anything. "Hunter, I ..." she began, unsure of what to say when it finally felt the silence had gone on too long.

He took this as a cue to continue. "Roxanne Elizabeth Hudson," he said, in a rehearsed voice. "Would you do me the honor of becoming my wife?"

Chapter Seventeen

The next time Roxanne could think clearly, she was standing alone on the cabin's front porch, clutching the blue ring box in her hand like some kind of flotation device. She knew she'd embarrassed Hunter when she'd fled the room, but he'd basically ambushed her. First, he'd shown up in Vermont. Then the dress. Then the news about Dahlia, and her designs, and Paris. It was more than she could handle at once.

Normally, Roxanne wasn't claustrophobic. But as soon as Hunter had asked her to marry him, each of the cabin's four walls had started closing. If she'd stayed in the room any longer, she would have eventually been crushed to death under the weight of his question and her family's penetrating gazes.

It didn't help that she couldn't answer him.

She couldn't believe he'd asked. Did he really expect her to say yes? None of this made sense. What was happening?

Outside in the cold night air, at least she could breathe again. Once her pulse returned to a more normal rhythm, she decided she needed to talk to someone—anyone—she could trust. At the moment, it was far preferable to being left with her own thoughts, which were basically just a mishmash of doubts and insecurity, her two worst enemies. Roxanne slid her arms into Maggie's borrowed coat and pulled her cell phone out of the pocket.

Five full bars stood on the upper corner of her iPhone screen, and Roxanne let out a sigh of relief. Finally, decent cell service.

Seconds later, her phone started to chime and ding as a list of notifications flooded the screen. The most recent alert told her Hunter had tagged her in a post. Roxanne swiped the post and saw a selfie of his smiling face holding the ring box open so every casual scroller would see the beautiful engagement ring in high resolution. The time stamp below the snap was from this morning. The caption read, *By the time she sees this, she'll have already said yes.*

Roxanne snorted. She *hadn't* said yes, but she hadn't exactly said no either. In fact, what she'd said before she'd made a hasty exit had been something along the lines of, "I need some air."

Roxanne closed the app. She debated opening up her inbox, but the count of unread emails waiting for her made her change her mind. One thing at a time. Not feeling like she had enough privacy to speak out loud, she opened up a new text conversation and quickly thumbed a message to Spencer.

MERRY CHRISTMAS EVE. Roxanne breathed a sigh of relief when she saw three flashing dots appear on the screen, signaling Spencer had begun his response.

You too, honey. I got your message—is everything okay?

Everything's fine. Sort of.

How's Martha and Snoop's?

Crowded. Hunter is here. And he proposed.

I'm sorry, he did WHAT?

YEAH. She could feel Spencer's tone through his text.

When?

Maybe five minutes ago.

Roxanne's finger tapped the side of her phone. He also broke the news about Paris. Did you know?

About the job or the proposal?

Either. Both.

Spencer's response dotted and then went flat. A millisecond later, his photo appeared on the screen, signaling an incoming video call.

When she answered the call, Spencer was standing on the terrace of his apartment, bundled up against the cold. His coat was unbuttoned, and she could hear upbeat holiday music playing loudly behind him. Trust Spencer to be partying on Christmas Eve.

"Roxanne, honey," he started without giving her time to say a proper hello. "Everyone knows about Paris. Ev-ery-one. It's taking over my inbox. But do you honestly think I wouldn't have said something if I knew about the *proposal?*"

He gasped at Roxanne's silence.

"You're *not* thinking of saying yes?"

"To Paris or the proposal?" She scoffed, icy breath billowing in front of her. "I don't know. Right now, nothing feels right." The truth rushed out. "I'm thrilled that Vivian and Dahlia loved my designs, it's just ... I don't know if *I* love them, you know. Couture isn't exactly my thing."

Spencer rolled his eyes. "I know you had your heart set on something closer to your original designs, but this is the opportunity of a lifetime—like, *literally* your dream come true. Besides, it's not like you can't move around once you get your foot in the door. Everyone starts somewhere. And we're celebrating when you get home, by the way. But I swear, that boy *never* misses an opportunity."

Roxanne scrunched her nose, caught off guard by the last. "What do you mean?"

Spencer patted down a stray strand of hair that had dared escape. He fixed her with his trademark snarky expression. "Honey, come on. You're smarter than that. You guys broke up, *again*, and then he suddenly shows up and proposes right after your career gets the green light and you're set to become the next big name in fashion?" He huffed. "Right, and I'm Beyoncé's long-lost brother."

She opened her mouth to interrupt, but Spencer kept talking before she could get a word in. "Look, I'm not saying he's riding your coattails or anything, but it sure would have been nice if the boy let you enjoy *you* for a second. You earned it."

"You're right." She hadn't wanted to admit it, even to herself, but the thought had crossed Roxanne's mind. Hunter was ambitious and obsessed with appearances, but was he really that shallow? In the end, it didn't matter. The very fact that she had to consider the possibility was all the answer she needed. Of course, he was.

"At least he brought home one of my dresses as a Christmas gift. That was sweet."

Spencer's eyes thinned into slits. "Which dress?"

Roxanne held the phone as far away from her as she could, daring a gust of winter air as she peeled open her coat to expose the garment underneath. "He brought it back with him from Madrid."

On the screen, Spencer's mouth formed an *oh*, his eyes

popping wide as he leaned in for closer inspection. "Oh, do not tell me he passed that off as his own idea," he exclaimed. "*Vivian* had that dress made for you as a congratulations gift. He probably got it from her when he popped in the office trying to hunt you down."

"Oh." There it was. Not only had Vivian given Hunter her parents' address in Vermont, but she'd handed over the dress, and he'd passed it off as his own. A sick feeling twisted in her stomach, the taste of acid rising up her throat.

Spencer clicked his teeth on the other end of the line. "I'm guessing he left out that part, though."

Roxanne snorted. "Yep."

"Well, it looks fantastic on you and that's the most important part," Spencer said. "You were *born* to wear red velvet."

"Thanks."

Spencer allowed a beat of silence for Roxanne to process, then, "So, what did you say?"

"I didn't say anything. I didn't know what to say. Still don't."

"You know, just because the boy has monumentally bad timing doesn't mean the proposal isn't genuine," Spencer tried, uncharacteristically optimistic. "Maybe he thought everything at once would be super exciting. He does like a good show."

Roxanne bit her lip. "Sure, so long as it's about it him."

Spencer's face crumbled into a conciliatory pout. "At least tell me he bought a spectacular ring?"

She lifted the Tiffany box to the screen.

"Boring," was Spencer's verdict.

Roxanne had to laugh. "Classic."

No, not classic. Bogart was classic. Hunter's ring was … *quaint.*

"So, I'm guessing no special deliveries by the big guy in red, then? Was kinda hoping you'd come home with a big, strapping mountain man," Spencer teased.

Mark's face bubbled to the top of Roxanne's thoughts. "Actually, I think I met one. It's not like that, though, but I've got a story for you when I get home."

"'It's not like that,'" Spencer mocked. "That's what you say when it's *exactly* like that. Spill the tea."

Spencer was still breathing into the screen when someone knocked softly from the other side of the cabin door. Holding her breath, Roxanne pulled it open, revealing Grandma Myrtle. She had a mug of cocoa in her hand, and a blanket laid across the lap of her wheelchair.

"Mind if I join you?" she asked.

"Of course, Grandma." Roxanne help guide her grandmother out onto the porch landing. "Spence, I'll call you back," she directed into the phone. She saw Spencer's eye roll as she ended the video feed.

"That boyfriend of yours is all in a tizzy," Grandma Myrtle said into her cocoa. "Haven't seen a man so upset since Nixon resigned."

Roxanne couldn't help but laugh. "Probably my fault. I don't think I had quite the reaction he was hoping for."

Myrtle clicked her teeth. "Well, that's his problem, not yours." She leveled an evaluating gaze at Roxanne, the frames of her glasses reflecting the glow of the lights strung on the porch eaves. "So, what are you going to tell him?"

Roxanne lowered herself onto the bench next to her grandmother's wheelchair, careful to smooth her dress out from under her. "I don't know. Three days ago I would have said yes. I would have doubted myself, but I would have said yes."

"A lot can change in a couple of days," her grandmother said wisely.

"Yeah," Roxanne agreed. She burrowed her head into the neck of Maggie's coat and tried hard not to think about Mark. A lot *could* change in three days. Maybe even Roxanne herself could change. She felt like a totally different person than she had been when she'd left the City. She was still the same old Roxanne, but it was almost as if she was awake in a way that she hadn't been before. Actually, that was it. She was the old Roxanne again, the one she'd been before she moved to New York and traded in her ideas for opportunities.

Myrtle laughed, took a long draw from her cocoa, and set the empty mug on her lap.

"Change is sometimes good, sometimes bad, but always constant, and it doesn't worry itself with timelines." The old woman cast a long, thoughtful look out into the night. "If something doesn't feel right, it's usually not. You know, when I first met your grandfather, I could have sworn I heard bells, I was so smitten. No rhyme or reason for it, but one look at Jimmy was enough to change the rest of my life."

"Bells?" Roxanne echoed. She remembered the bells she'd been hearing for the past couple of days. They'd started right at the moment of her accident and ended the moment Mark had walked away. But a few days wasn't enough time to fall in love with someone, was it? The Roxanne of last week would have said no way, but today's Roxanne wasn't so sure. She recalled the way Mark's lips had felt against hers under the mistletoe in the snow and realized she would be happy if that was the last first kiss she ever had. Maybe there was something to all Mark's hokum about Christmas magic after all. It sure had made a believer out of her.

"Bells," Grandma Myrtle confirmed, her voice dropping to a whisper as she fingered her wedding band. "Used to hear them jingling every time he kissed me," she said with a sad smile. "Jimmy's been gone for over ten years, and sometimes, when I miss him the most, I think I can still hear them. Especially on nights like tonight."

"Why tonight?" Roxanne asked.

"Because it's Christmas." Myrtle laughed, as if it were obvious. "The season of love—love of the deepest kind." She motioned at the box in Roxanne's hand. "Not the kind that can be bought in a store, either. The kind what makes Christmas so magical is in here."

She placed her hand over Roxanne's heart.

"You're a smart lady, Grandma Myrtle," Roxanne said, reaching up to cover her grandmother's hand with hers.

Myrtle laughed. "Oh, honey, when you get to be my age you can't help but be smart. You've had a whole lot of life to put behind you and learned a lot of lessons along the way. Some are easy, some are hard, but either way, you're going to learn them, like it or not."

Roxanne put her face into her hands and mumbled, "What would you do if you were me, Grandma? Would you say yes to a man you weren't sure you really loved, or if he really loved you, because it was easy, and everybody was expecting you to? Would you move halfway around the world to chase an opportunity, even if it was different than the one you'd dreamed of?" She thought of her Plain Jane designs, of women like Andrea Steiner, who had let someone else's idea of beauty steal her own, and girls like Clara Costa, who had yet to be told they had to look and dress a certain way to be beautiful. Could she really sacrifice her vision to build her career on the back of stuff like that? "What if there was something on the inside, something little but noisy, trying to tell you to do something different? Would you listen, even if it was crazy?"

Grandma Myrtle leaned forward. A bright glint in her eye reflected the moonlight, and for a brief moment, Roxanne caught a glimpse of the woman Myrtle might have been a long, long time ago.

"Sweetheart, if I were your age again, I'd do it *all*. This is your life, and your choice, but I'll tell you one thing, honey child. If there's music in your heart, listen to it. That's something you don't want to miss."

Right then, Roxanne knew she couldn't marry Hunter any more than she could give up on her dreams—her real ones, even if they were quaint and plain to others. And for the first time since she'd stepped into her family's cabin, sitting on the front porch holding her grandmother's hand in the dark, the sound of sleigh bells filled her ears.

Chapter Eighteen

For the rest of the night, and well into the wee hours of the morning, Roxanne sat with her grandmother, both women lost in thought about love lost and gained and holiday magic. By the time they went back into the cabin, they were nearly frozen and it was almost dawn. Everyone else had gone off to bed without them, and the first rays of Christmas Day would soon light up the sky. They hadn't seen Santa come on his annual errand, but their hearts were full just the same.

Roxanne helped Grandma Myrtle settle into her bed, then tiptoed down the end of the hallway to her room. Hunter's eyelids flickered when she inched the bedroom door open. He sat up, rubbed his hands through his hair, and shot her an accusatory look dulled by sleep.

"You left me hanging last night, babe."

"I'm sorry. It was a lot at once. I needed to think."

He patted the bed beside him, and she sat, although she kept as close to the edge of the bed as possible. "You didn't answer my question."

Roxanne was not ready for the conversation that was coming,

but it had to happen anyway. Her mind was made up, even if her heart still hurt. "I know."

"It's okay," Hunter said. "Maybe it wasn't the best time. There's no hurry. We don't have to get married anytime soon. We can have a long engagement, call each other fiancé for so long it gets on everyone's nerves. Think about it, and—"

"I don't need to think about it, Hunter," Roxanne interrupted, raising her hand so he'd stop talking. "I can't marry you. What we have—what we *had*—it was good once. Now, I think we'd just be going through the motions, both of us planning our next steps and sort of pulling the other one along with us. It wouldn't be right. I'm sorry, but my answer is no." She set the ring box on the empty space of bed between them.

Hunter blinked a few times, as if it would help him digest her words. Finally, with a deep sigh, he asked, "Is it the ring? I can buy you a bigger one."

"It's not the ring."

They were silent for a few moments, and Hunter gave a frustrated sigh and leaned back into the pillows. "I can't say I'm not disappointed. I love you, Roxanne."

"I love you, too, but it's not the kind of love I want. I want … I want bells."

He looked confused, but she didn't explain. She knew Hunter, and he wouldn't understand.

"Hey, one more thing. What really happened with Andrea Steiner in Madrid?"

Hunter blinked. "Is that what this is about? Nothing ever happened between me and her, or anyone else, if that's what you're worried about. Not once. I swear."

"No, it's not that. I just need to know, was it seriously food poisoning?"

"Oh." Hunter's brow furrowed as he tried to connect the dots. "No, you were right. Andrea checked into some kind of rehab when we got back. I guess the pressure was getting to her. Why? What's that got to do with anything?"

"And the dress," she went on. "Did Vivian give it to you to give me?"

Hunter flinched. "Come on, babe. I—"

"And," Roxanne cut in, hearing the answer in the response he didn't say, "did you decide to bring it to me before or after you'd heard about Dahlia's offer? I saw the picture you posted of the engagement ring on social media—this morning." She waved her phone as evidence. "Finally got enough cell service to catch up on things."

"What does it matter, Rox?" Hunter shot back, impatience finally wearing through his carefully polished veneer. "It's your dress, your design. Yes, it was a happy coincidence I was able to get it, but it was a *sign*, babe. We're meant to be together. This is our next big break—you working with Paris's elite on your couture designs, and I'll be right by your side."

"So it was all about appearances."

Hunter raked his fingers through his hair in agitation but didn't deny it.

Roxanne nodded. "So you know, I'm not just turning you down. I'm not going to take Dahlia D'Arcy up on her offer, either."

Hunter's eyes went wide. "What? Why? Designing has been your dream for longer than I've known you. If it's me, we can end things peacefully. Professionally. It doesn't have to be a thing.

Don't turn Dahlia down just because you don't want to marry me."

Roxanne laughed, not surprised Hunter would somehow find a way to make himself part of an equation that never included him as a variable. Still, it might have been the most selfless thing he'd ever said to her. "I'm turning down Dahlia because if I go to France, I'll be working on my own designs, but it won't be the kind of designs I want to make. Instead I'll be designing clothes that make women like Andrea feel un-beautiful, and I couldn't live with myself then. At *Divine* I have the opportunity to do something different, to change things—flip the script in fashion. I can work to help make women feel beautiful again, even if they aren't a size zero with perfect skin. Even if they eat pie for breakfast."

She could tell Hunter was deeply confused, but it didn't matter. Leaving him to riddle out his own conclusions, she stood from the bed and wriggled the zipper of her dress down, then slipped on the only pair of blue jeans she'd brought with her. She pulled an old sweatshirt from her teenage wardrobe over her head, amazed it still fit, wiped her faded makeup from her face, and pulled her hair up into a messy ponytail.

"And you think Vivian is going to keep you at *Divine* if you turn down Dahlia?" Hunter laughed, now looking at her as if he thought she'd lost her mind. "You turn this down and your career in fashion is over."

"No, it's not," she said. "Vivian gave me my own column because I have a voice, and I intend to use it." She didn't look in the mirror as she stuffed her feet into Maggie's borrowed snow boots and laced them up, then pulled the arms of the coat over her shoulders.

"You have somewhere to be?" Hunter didn't bother to hide the fact he was miffed.

"As a matter of fact, I do."

"Don't expect me to be here when you get back," Hunter snapped. "I've got other options, you know. There are a lot of women who wouldn't turn me down. I'm not going to wait around for you to come to your senses, Roxanne."

Roxanne tossed the words over her shoulder. "That's too bad," she said, "because I think I finally have."

Chapter Nineteen

uckily, the morning was crisp and clear, and Roxanne remembered the way back to Mark's cabin. She grabbed the keys to her father's old pickup from the bowl where he kept them in the kitchen, wrote a small note of apology that promised she'd return soon, and said a silent prayer she'd remember how to drive a stick shift.

She stalled out once or twice before she got the hang of it, but in a few minutes, she was moving smoothly over the snow, which had hardened overnight into something more navigable. The tracks from the snowcat's tires were still visible, and Roxanne used them as a guide as she traced her steps back the way they'd come the previous day, toward the comfortable little cottage Mark kept a few miles away from her parents' place.

Along the way, she passed her BMW, and just as Mark had described, the car gave no indication it had been in an accident at all. Roxanne tapped the brakes and slowed to a crawl as she passed. It was covered in snow but otherwise looked perfect—as if she'd simply pulled off the side of the road, parked, and walked away. Yet, she was sure something had dashed out in front of her to make her spin out of control.

Roxanne shrugged and kept driving. Maybe it *had* been Santa.

With every mile, her heart beat faster, and though it was a short drive, by the time the cabin came into view, she'd exhausted every calming tactic she knew, and her pulse had reached a crescendo.

When she was close enough to the cabin to walk but far enough away that she hoped Mark wouldn't hear the rumble of the truck's engine, Roxanne pulled to a stop, secured the brake, and killed the motor. She inhaled a deep breath of air for courage and tried to talk herself out of starting the truck back up and taking off. She had made the decision to drive to Mark's and then done it, but she hadn't actually thought about what she would say when she got there. Would he even want to see her? Did he feel the same way? What if he hadn't heard the same bells she had? She might be walking headfirst into a collision with humiliation, and it made her stomach churn thinking about it.

Roxanne took a few deep breaths, stoking her courage like oxygen on a fire. She opened the driver's side door and charged toward the cabin. She took the few front steps in a bound, then rapped on the door, pressing her ear to the wood to listen to the sounds of shuffling inside.

"Hang on, old man."

She heard Mark speaking to Bogie on the other side of the door, and the sound of glassware clinking. In her mind, she saw Mark relaxed on his sofa, a mug of cinnamon-scented coffee in one hand. Maybe he had been reading, or maybe staring silently into the fire. The thought made her warm.

"Do you believe in fate?" Roxanne blurted out the moment

the door cracked open and Mark's face appeared in the doorway. She ignored the fact that he wasn't wearing a shirt and his flannel pajama bottoms were hanging dangerously low on his hips.

"Roxy?"

Mark's voice was full of disbelief as Roxanne watched through the crack in the door as he pulled on a fleece jacket. He zipped it up partway, then rubbed his hands on his arms to temper the sting of the frosty outside air. Roxanne could hear a roaring fire cracking behind him. He opened the door and stepped out, then pulled the door closed behind him but didn't latch it.

"What are you doing here? Is everything okay?"

Mark's voice was all concern, but Roxanne waved it away.

"Do you?" she pressed.

"Do I believe in fate?" he echoed, crinkling his nose.

"Yeah," she said, sucking in a deep breath of air. "Like, fate bringing two people together. I mean, I didn't even want to come to Vermont for Christmas. And then I did, and I was almost to the cabin, and then I had my accident. I don't know what happened, and the more I think about it, the more I don't think anything actually did. But, if it hadn't been for that, I wouldn't have met you, and I wouldn't have ..." Her voice trailed off as words failed her. She was rambling, and he wasn't saying anything, and she was starting to have a hard time not feeling totally silly. "You know," she finished lamely.

The ghost of a smile appeared on Mark's face, and he closed the distance between them. "Are you asking me if I believe in love at first sight?"

She sighed. Shivered. Maybe this *was* stupid, but Mark's tone wasn't condescending. It was something else entirely—low and breathy and inviting.

"Yes. No. Maybe—" She shook her head, arguing with herself. "I don't know. I just know when I'm with you I see myself more clearly, and now that I've seen that version of me, I don't want to lose sight of her—and I don't want to lose sight of you."

"What about Mr. Fancy Watch at the cabin? Your high-profile life in New York? I can't give that to you, Roxy. Not even close."

"Honestly, I don't think it's what I want anymore. I don't think it ever was." She grimaced. "I spent so much time creating my life around this image of everything I thought perfection was, that I stopped actually trying to be happy. I forgot why I wanted to go into fashion to begin with, and somehow being with you the past couple of days has made me remember all the things I had forgotten and forget all the things I thought I was so certain about. Is that crazy?"

She was still talking, but Mark's arms had found their way around her. He was looking down at her in his patient way, and a smile was flickering on the corner of his lips.

"Crazy?" He laughed. "Probably. And to answer your original question, I don't know if I believe in love at first sight."

Roxanne felt a piece of her heart break. This had been such a bad idea.

"But I do believe in the magic of Christmas," he continued, "and finding you has been the best gift I could have ever received."

Hope sprung in Roxanne's chest. "Me?"

"You. The holidays are kind of lonely around here, and I had come to accept that, but now it's even lonelier with you gone."

"I don't want to be gone. Not from myself, not anymore. And not from you."

The green of Mark's eyes glinted and a warm feeling flooded her, rising up through her feet until it reached the tip of her nose. "So, what are you saying?"

Roxanne thought about it. "I think you might have been right before, when I said we were polar opposites."

"I have heard opposites attract."

"They *complement* each other," Roxanne corrected. "Sweet and savory. Cheese and wine. Martha and Snoop."

Mark cocked his head to the side, eyebrow raised in question, and Roxanne shook the analogy away, not wanting to waste time explaining. She moved closer to her point. "Summer and winter, Vermont and New York City."

"Ah, I see."

"So, maybe we can test it out? See if the bells keep ringing after Santa goes back to the North Pole?" Roxanne bit her lip as she waited for his response.

Mark was holding her now, and as the feel of his arms around her filled her body with warmth, the sound of sleigh bells sang once more in her ears as if in answer. "I'd have to check with Bogie, but the old fella's pretty fond of you so I think he'd give us his blessing. Maybe I'll even enjoy those summer concerts in Central Park, so long as you promise to get a better set of snow tires before you head back up the mountain." He gave her a squeeze. "I'm all in, Roxy."

"And what if Bogie disapproves?" Roxanne shot back, joining in on the joke as the old dog stuck his snout through the small space between the door and the threshold. He must have heard his name. "He might not hear the bells like we do."

"Well …" Mark pretended to consider the question. "Poor guy's pretty much deaf anyway, so I'd be willing to take the risk."

Roxanne reached one hand out to give the old dog's ear a tender scratch. She closed her eyes and let herself get lost in Mark's arms with her head against his chest. When she opened her eyes again, she started to laugh.

"What's so funny?"

"Look up." Hanging above their heads, in a bright burst of green and red among the wooden rafters of the porch, was a large bulb of mistletoe.

"What in the world? I swear I didn't hang that there." Mark's voice was incredulous.

"Must be another bit of Christmas magic," Roxanne mused, angling her head toward his.

"Well." He shrugged and his body hugged hers. He looked at her, and the sound of bells was distinct now—as if Santa himself had just landed his sleigh on the lawn behind her back. "Rules are rules. Are you up for another kiss under the mistletoe?" he asked, touching his palm to the underside of her jaw.

"I am."

A deep breath later Mark's lips were on hers.

"How about that Christmas dinner?" Roxanne asked when it was over, this time without the slightest amount of hesitation. She motioned backward at her father's truck, parked crookedly in his Mark's drive. "I'd love to introduce you to my Grandma Myrtle. I'll drive."

Mark laughed and kissed her again. "I wouldn't miss it. Let me grab another pie."

Afterword

The statistic Roxanne quoted to Hunter—that over 62% of models have been asked to lose weight or change their shape or size for the sake of their careers—is, at least as of the publication of a 2017 study conducted by Rodgers, Ziff, Lowy, Yu, and Austin, true.

The full research, which was published in the *International Journal of Eating Disorders*, explored the appearance pressures experienced by fashion models and evaluated recent legislative policy changes meant to address harmful practices in the fashion/modeling industries. Rodgers, et al.'s findings, though limited, highlight the reality that fashion models indeed experience high levels of pressure from their agencies to lose weight and maintain a very low body weight—sometimes beyond what is normally considered to be medically healthy.

In another study, researchers Zancu and Enea conducted a systematic literature review on eating disorders among fashion models. With a very low number of appropriate studies conducted on the subject between 1980 and 2015—seven, in total—Zancu and Enea concluded that not only is available research scarce, but what does exist cannot be generalized and fails to clarify the matter of disordered eating among professional models.

In short: we don't know enough, but we do know there is a relationship between the fashion industry and eating disorders—and it generally isn't positive.

Anyone familiar with mainstream advertising and the fashion industry-at-large may not be shocked to learn that fashion plays a critical role in the development and widespread dissemination of body imagery. Nor would it be any great surprise that the "thin-ideal" is chief among these images, or that such images are sometimes created at the cost of the fashion models' health, as well as the health of the wider population. These images are even more problematic among adolescent girls, who, routinely and pervasively exposed to such images, have higher associations of risk for eating disorders among other mental and emotional traumas.

Even with the shift toward body positivity, such pervasive ideals of beauty are not quickly forgotten, and the "thin-ideal" remains the norm. Lately, even the concept of body positivity has come under criticism, charged with pushing a tone of "toxic positivity." While the concept of self-love and acceptance of one's body is necessary and transformative, it often overlooks more in-depth exploration of the complex problems and negative feelings that affect one's ability to truly accept their bodies. Beauty, after all, is in the eye of the beholder, and there is truth in the adage that each of us are our own worst critics.

In light of this, artists and icons like Lizzo and Jameela Jamil are now championing what's called "body neutrality," a movement that celebrates gratefulness over self-love. Like anything, this mantra is not without its flaws, and some have noted a degree of able-bodied privilege associated with choosing to be grateful for how a body functions, versus how it looks, particularly if one's body doesn't function in ways that others' do.

However, while academic inquiry and conversations surrounding body imagery, self-love, and healthy eating habits both within the fashion industry and without continues, the message I would like to bring to my readers is a simple one: embrace yourself. It isn't my place, nor anyone else's, to tell you what your experience with your body should be. How to feel about it. Whether or not you accept it, or whether it adheres to beauty standards, real or imagined.

Loving your body is a journey, not a goal, and you are so much more than the sum of your parts. I encourage you to embrace yourself, flaws and all, and see the beauty that is uniquely, unequivocally, unabashedly you. Give yourself the grace to be imperfect, permission to be a work in progress. Eat your pie—metaphorical or otherwise—for breakfast.

Further information on the studies cited can be found in the following:

Levine, M. P., & Murnen, S. K. (2009). Everybody knows that mass media are/are not [pick one] a cause of eating disorders": A critical review of evidence for a causal link between media, negative body image, and disordered eating in females. *Journal of Social and Clinical Psychology*, 28(9).

Rodgers, R. F., Ziff, S., Lowy, A. S., Yu, K., & Austin, S. B. (2017). Results of a strategic science study to inform policies targeting extreme thinness standards in the fashion industry. *The International Journal of Eating Disorders*, 50(3), 284–292.

Zancu, S. A., & Enea, V. (2017). Eating disorders among fashion models: A systematic review of the literature. *Eating and Weight Disorders: EWD*, 22(3), 395–405.

RECIPES

Maple Cream Pie

Ingredients
- 1 premade deep-dish pie crust, baked and cooled
- 3 cups half & half
- ½ cup maple syrup
- 4 large egg yolks
- 1 cup brown sugar
- 1/3 cup cornstarch, sifted
- ¼ teaspoon salt
- 1 teaspoon vanilla extract
- ¼ teaspoon maple flavor, optional
- Whipped cream, to top

Method
1. Mix half & half, maple syrup, egg yolks, brown sugar, cornstarch, and salt in a medium pan. Cook over medium heat, stirring constantly, until mixture thickens and boils (about 10 to 12 minutes).
2. Remove from heat and add in maple flavor and vanilla.
3. Pour the filling into cooled pie crust shell.
4. Refrigerate for at least 4 hours, preferably overnight.
5. Top with whip cream—and dig in!

Snowballs

Ingredients

- 1 cup butter
- 4 tablespoons powdered sugar
- 1 tablespoon water
- 2 tablespoons vanilla
- 2 cups flour, sifted
- 1/3 teaspoon salt
- 1 cup chopped pecans, optional

Method

1. Preheat oven to 325 and prepare cookie sheets.
2. Cream together butter and sugar.
3. Add water, vanilla, flour, salt, and pecans. Mix well.
4. Pinch off bits of dough and roll about into 1-2-inch balls. Place onto cookie sheet.
5. Bake for 20-30 minutes, or until slightly brown.
6. Roll in powdered sugar while still warm. Wait to cool— and enjoy!

ACKNOWLEDGEMENTS

To Toni Miller, for humoring me with my very first experiment with holiday romance stories—and for Roxanne. Who would have thought the two of us would have come up with such a sweet story?

To Italia Gandolfo, Liana Gardner, and the editorial and design teams at Rosewind Books, for always believing in my work and giving it the love and attention it needs to shine.

To Finn, for hours spent curled beneath my feet, listening to me type, and who gives me so much love I can't help but put some of it on the page.

To Stephen, aka Hot Pocket. My goodness, I don't have enough words to write my appreciation for how much joy you bring to my life. Thank you.

And, of course, to maple syrup pie.

ABOUT THE AUTHOR

 Lindy Miller is an award-winning author of feel-good love stories full of sweet moments and happy endings. She believes the best time to fall in love is during the holidays, preferably over a cup of warm tea or a delicious pastry—two things she can't get enough of.

Lindy is represented by Gandolfo Helin & Fountain Literary Management and supported by Meryl Moss Media.

Member Romantic Novelist Association (RNA) and Romance Writers of America (RWA).

www.GlitterAndGravedust.com